SAVED BY THE HITMAN

ALEXIS ABBOTT

USA TODAY & WALL STREET JOURNAL BESTSELLING AUTHOR

This book is intended for sale to Adult Audiences only. It contains sexually explicit scenes and graphic language. All sexually active characters in this work are over the age of 18.

ISBN-13: **978-1545531341**
ISBN-10: **154553134X**

CHAPTER 1 - CHERRY

I should have worn better shoes.

Garden State, my ass, I think bitterly to myself as I awkwardly stumble through the warehouse in the dark. This morning when I woke up in my hotel room in Newark, I sleepily opened my shiny New Yorker suitcase to peruse my wardrobe options, all of which are also distinctly New Yorker in style. That is to say, they are much better suited to a strut down Fifth Avenue than a tromp through the muddy backroads of New Jersey.

Shoes, especially.

I am accustomed to sharp stilettos, suede ankle boots, and fire-engine-red pumps. None of which are particularly appropriate for a day of exploring the site of my father's death. This warehouse is dark, dank, and definitely a stark departure from my usual haunts. I mean, I *am* a journalist, so you might expect me to be used to running around in unusual places, sniffing out the next big story. But because my deadbeat mom was so generous and considerate as to land me with a name like Cherry LaBeau, I've never exactly been on the shortlist for the Pulitzer Prize.

In fact, I've been lucky to score the cushy, inconsequential, lighthearted pieces they've handed off to me in the past. I've been a fashion blogger, a who's-who editorialist, and a celebrity gossip generator for several years, and it's paid fairly well — which is to say not much by most standards. Well enough to keep me housed, fed, and decked out in (admittedly out-of-season) designer clothes in the very expensive city of the Big Apple all this time.

It would almost be a dream job.

Except that it's the opposite of anything I've ever dreamed of.

Despite the girly, tongue-in-cheek name on my birth certificate, I'd like to think there's nothing very frivolous about me. Sure, I write the puff pieces they assign me and I wear the knock-off Carrie Bradshaw outfits they expect me to. I sign my ridiculous name with a flourish, and I dot my "i's" with a heart. But beneath all that superficiality is a real, hard-hitting journalist, just itching to break free and finally write something of substance.

And it's what my father would have wanted for me.

"People are going to judge you for your name, sweetheart," he told me when I was eighteen and heading off to university to get my journalism degree. "But that just means you gotta work that much harder. Make them take you seriously. Be so good at what you do that they're forced to say your name with respect."

Standing in my inappropriate high-heeled boots in this dripping, musty warehouse, I have to bite my lip to keep back the tears threatening to sting in my eyes. I can't be weak. I can't let my emotions cripple me. I've got to be strong like Dad was. Especially if I'm going to find out what happened to him… and who killed him.

It's safer to think about my shoes, something silly and non-consequential. It helps keep my mind off how much I miss my dad. The only family I have — had — left. Now it's just me, and I swore at his funeral that I'd make him proud in the afterlife.

It's autumn here in Bayonne, New Jersey, and even deep inside this warehouse I can feel the occasional cool draft rippling through. I shiver and wrap my black trench coat more tightly around myself. This place is near enough to the coast that I could probably just run to the beach from here if I wanted to. But not yet. As tempting as it would be to just plop down on the Jersey Shore and let the salty fresh air mix with my tears, I didn't come here for that purpose. I have something more important to do. I'm on a mission.

So I take a deep breath and try my best to walk lightly through the warehouse. This is easier said than done because my damn high-fashion boots are about as quiet as a foghorn, and the vast emptiness of this building causes my footfalls to echo slightly. Still, I doubt anyone else would come here — not since it was designated a crime scene.

Right?

After all, as far as I know nobody even owns it anymore. It's sat out here on a muddy dirt road, abandoned, for so long that the original owners have probably died. I don't know what this place was even used for. Except for murdering people in secret.

There's that God-awful sting of tears again and I angrily swallow back the lump in my throat. I've come too far and risked too much to let myself be done in by my own stupid emotions. I can mourn later. Now, it's time to buckle down and get the scoop.

I take a few more cautious steps before I'm distracted by what sounds like voices.

My blood runs cold, but I assure myself it's got to be the draft rolling down the empty aisles, playing tricks on my spooked mind. There's nobody here, I'm sure of it. Nobody but me.

But when I take another step I hear a distinctive shout.

I freeze up immediately, my eyes going wide. *Oh no,* I think fearfully, *maybe it's the cops coming by to check and make sure nobody's disturbing the crime scene*. But then again, they told me the forensics team already got all the information they needed, that the clean-up crew came through and cleared it all up long before I arrived. If there's nothing else left to investigate, why would the cops be here?

My heart sinks into my gut.

Unless they're not cops.

Feeling nauseous but strangely exhilarated, I lean into a massive metal shelf and strain my ears, trying to be utterly still and silent. I hold my breath and close my eyes, shutting out all extraneous sensory information so I can focus in on the voices. Sure enough, I'm able to make out the distant muttering of what seems to be a group of men.

A group? My heart starts to race as a sense of genuine danger starts to dawn on me. What am I doing here? I'm not a cop! I'm not a private investigator! I don't have a gun or any kind of weapon at all, and even if I did, I would have no clue how to use it. I'm just a desperately curious, frightened fashion writer who has dropped herself smack-dab in the middle of what could potentially be some kind of criminal lair.

Stupid, stupid, stupid! I scold myself inwardly. What kind of idiot goes sleuthing around a murder scene unarmed and alone?

Holding my breath so tightly that my chest starts to ache, I can finally pick out a few choice words drifting over from across the massive warehouse: *Cops. Information. Suspects.*

Finally I'm forced to exhale and inhale sharply, letting the damp air fill my lungs.

What on earth have I stumbled into here? What if these men are dangerous? I'm not prepared for a fight — hell, in these shoes I'm not even prepared for a quick escape. But something tells me I can't turn back now. I've only been in this warehouse for five or six minutes, after an hour and a half of driving to get here. And who knows — the men talking might just reveal pertinent information about my father's death. I can't risk giving into my fear and bolting out of here now — not when things are just starting.

Besides, if I really want to make my late father proud, I've got to stop hiding behind frilly, innocuous fluff articles and blog posts, and start really getting into the nitty-gritty world of journalism. And that means embracing danger, walking bravely into the line of fire just for a shot at capturing that most elusive and beautiful prize: the truth.

Still, I can't help but gasp in shock at the loud yell I hear next: "What do they know? What have they done?"

I cover my mouth to stifle my heavy panting. I'm so frightened by now that I've got goosebumps prickling up along my arms and legs, even under warm layers of clothing. It's a man's harsh voice I hear, almost a growl. His tone is accusatory and laced with venom. He sounds mean. Scary. Cruel.

I wait for the reply, which comes after a few tense moments.

"I don't know! I swear! Don't you think I'd tell you if — "

There's a loud cracking sound and then a man's pained yelp. I crouch down in fear, suddenly wanting to make myself smaller, less detectable. This certainly doesn't sound like a civil conversation. It sounds like something dark is going down.

"Get up," orders a third man. His voice is very deep, his tone controlled. He sounds calmer, and yet more commanding. Even though he isn't as loud as the other two, his voice carries the long distance, with an impressive resonance that sends a shiver down my spine, even with just those two words. I feel the insatiable need to see what he looks like, to put a face to the compelling voice.

Against my better judgment and every straining fiber of self-preservation in my body, I begin to creep along toward the voices. But my shoes — damn, useless pieces of crap — are too loud. I just can't bear it. They might overhear me if I keep on this way. So, even though it pains me, I carefully slip them off my feet to carry them instead. As my toes, clad only in thin hosiery, touch the frigid, filthy floor, I grimace with disgust. Would it really have killed me to invest in a pair of sneakers before driving all the way out here? I have a lot to learn. This isn't a Scooby Doo episode — I can't run around in Daphne-esque heels and perfectly-styled hair if I'm going to make this work. Especially because the monsters I'm dealing with aren't fake.

They're murderers.

I can feel it in my soul. These guys in the warehouse have got to be related to my father's death in some way or another. It can't possibly be a coincidence that they're here right now yelling about cops and stuff, when just a week ago my father's life was snuffed out in the exact same location. I grit my teeth and force myself to ignore how gross the ground is beneath my feet as I move slowly, cautiously along toward the men.

"My associate gave you an order! Get on your feet, ya bastard!" commands the first voice I heard earlier. There's the rustle of something like metal dragging on the concrete floor and I furrow my brows trying to figure out what the hell it might be. Then it hits me with a jolt to my heart: chains. It's the sound of metal chains clinking and rolling across the floor.

What the hell? I crouch down even further as I continue to make my way closer. Even though everything just got a million levels more bizarre and horrifying, I feel totally drawn to the sounds of their voices. I have got to figure out what's going on, even if doing so thrusts me directly into the lap of danger.

Besides, with my father gone, I don't exactly have anything else to lose.

"I don't know anythin' about it, man! *Nichego*!" exclaims the second voice. He's the one being interrogated, the one whose voice is wavering with fear. As I come closer, I peer around the ceiling-high metal storage shelves to see the three men only about fifty yards away from me. My jaw drops at the sight.

There's a man with both arms chained to the floor, metal links around his wrists keeping him bound to about a ten foot reach. He's drenched in sweat and his eyes are nearly bugging out of his head, he's so scared. He looks like a skeevy rat of a man, with receding, blondish hair, scrawny limbs, and a long, hooked nose. He's wearing a polo shirt and cargo pants which are much too large for him, and he's kneeling on one knee, looking up at the two other guys with desperate, imploring eyes.

"Bullshit!" snarls the first voice, which I see now belongs to a tall, wiry, brown-haired guy in a light blue shirt and khakis. If not for the rolled-up sleeves and combative stance, he would look for all the world like a harmless Sunday school teacher or something. That image is shattered completely when he reels back and lands a solid kick to the chained guy's calves.

The rat-like man falls on his hands and knees, buckling over in pain as he yells out, "*Klyanus*! I have nothing to say! It's not one of ours!"

"I can't abide a liar," says the third man. A shiver runs down my spine as I realize he's the one with the resonant voice. He's even taller than the blue-shirt guy, with broad shoulders, and very dark hair. Even from here I can see the muscles tight underneath his dark jeans and black, short-sleeved shirt. There's a thick black leather jacket crumpled behind him on the floor, as though he recently took it off. Then I notice that there's a similar-looking jacket lying vaguely behind the blue-shirt guy, too. Weird.

"Hear that, *zasranec*? Your lies won't be tolerated!" shouts blue-shirt. He pulls back for another kick but the cowering rat-man shrinks away instinctively.

The man in black raises a hand to stop them, his other hand rubbing at his temple.

"Maybe we're going about this the wrong way, eh?" he begins, that deep voice filling my brain like intoxicating cigar smoke. "Perhaps you'd respond better to positive reinforcement."

The rat-man perks up immediately, his sniveling face peeking out from behind his arms. He nods rapidly and begins to stand back up to take a few steps toward black-shirt. "*Da, da, moy drug*! What is your offer?"

Blue-shirt gestures angrily toward him, giving his associate a scathing, indignant glare. "You want to make a deal with this slug, Leon? Come on! Let's just bash his ugly face in!"

"Quiet, Lukas!" black-shirt commands, holding up one finger to silence him. So his name had to be Leon. The name made me shiver.

Blue-shirt — Lukas — backs down, crossing his arms over his chest and rolling his eyes. Then Leon moves in on the rat-man and says, "What can you tell me about what happened here? How much do you really know?"

Fidgeting nervously and glancing back and forth between Leon and Lukas, the rat-man stammers, "I-I don't know much, b-but I could give you some names of those who m-might have information for you."

Leon snaps his fingers and the rat-man flinches. "Well? Spill!"

"F-first I need to know what you're gonna give me in return."

Lukas rounds on him furiously, snatching him up by the collar. "How about letting you leave this shithole with your miserable life? That good enough?"

Terrified, the rat-man starts to ramble very quickly. "I-I heard from my cousin Vic that his *podruga's* sister knows a guy who got p-picked up by the *politsiya* about the LaBeau case!"

At the mention of my own last name I let out a startled gasp and drop my boots to the floor with a resounding, echoing clunk. My eyes go wide as all three men swivel around toward the sound — toward me.

"What the hell was that?" snarls Lukas, looking around with narrowed eyes.

"Help! Help!" the rat-man starts squealing, desperately thinking I might be a cop or someone here to rescue him from his chained interrogation.

"*Zatk'nis, mu'dak*!" roars Lukas, jabbing a right hook into the rat-man's face.

"Who's there?" calls out Leon, walking briskly toward me, squinting.

Oh no.

He's going to find me. I'm going to die. They're going to chain me up and beat the hell out of me like they're doing to the rat-man. It's all over.

Just then, my fight or flight instinct kicks in. Flight takes the reins.

With a terrified little squeal I stand up, tuck my boots under my arm, and bolt away as fast as my nearly-bare feet can carry me, my heart pounding in my ears.

"Stop! Stop right there!" Leon shouts, his voice running chills down my tingling limbs. I can hear his heavy footsteps quickening behind me. He's chasing me.

"Boss?" Lukas yells.

"Stay back! I've got this!" Leon calls back in response.

He's got this.

He's got *me*.

CHAPTER 2 - CHERRY

My head is pounding and my entire body aches, my legs having gone numb from running so far, so fast, in the cold air. My feet are frozen by this point, my toes totally without feeling. I've still got my boots tucked up under my arm, which is trembling but paralyzed in a kind of vice grip. The muddy, slushy earth beneath me splatters and smacks with every frantic step I take. I have not dared to look behind me, and I can't hear much beyond the booming of my heart beat and the blood rushing in my ears. I am not a runner by any means, and in fact my gym membership card was little more than a shiny, colorful little decoration on my dresser back at my apartment in the city. I went a few times, but it was never a priority for me. The work I did, the kind of profile I kept, required me to be pretty and slim, but certainly not buff.

So this is probably the most physical exercise I've had in years. And it shows.

My lungs are in constant pain, causing me to wince with every labored breath. I don't even know how long I've been running now. It could be fifteen minutes or it could be five hours — either way, I cannot wipe the fear out of my mind that my would-be attacker is just a few steps behind the whole way. I hope, vaguely, that I am running in the direction of help. Out here, in as close to the middle of nowhere as you can possibly get in the industrial state of New Jersey, it's hard to find your way back to the road. At first, I took off into the woods, not thinking clearly enough to have a real destination in mind. But slowly, cautiously, I've made my way back in a loop toward where I think I parked my rental car.

Somewhere in the back of my brain, there's a shrill voice screaming at me. *How could you possibly lose your car? What kind of idiot are you?*

But at last the glint of something like polished metal flashes in the watery sunlight just ahead and my heart soars.

A sleek, unobtrusive, little green Ford Focus. My rental car. Thank God!

Somehow I manage to wrangle my aching, half-responsive arm into the back left pocket of my jeans to fish out the keys. With all the momentum I've been building up, I all but slam into the driver's side door, shaking violently as I fumble to fit the key into the door. Finally I allow myself to look around, my eyes blinking and wide as I scan the area for my pursuer. He's nowhere in sight, but that does little to satisfy my fear.

"Come on, come on," I mumble nervously. Then the key wiggles into the hole and I turn it to unlock the door and fling it open. "A-ha!"

A-ha? What are you, a magician? I think to myself in annoyance. I jab the key into the ignition and turn the engine over, immediately throwing the car into reverse and peeling out in a sharp, backward semi-circle before switching to drive and jerking forward. With my basically-bare foot shoving the gas pedal down to the floor, the Focus plows down along the dirt road I took to get here, barreling away from the warehouse, away from this nightmare.

The trees blow past, leaning narrowly into the pathway as though half-heartedly trying to guard me from leaving. As I drive along at a definitely-illegal speed, I notice that my toes are regaining feeling — and that the thin hosiery has worn through. It probably disintegrated some ten or fifteen minutes ago from being pounded into the wet, rocky ground. Another pair of pantyhose ruined in the name of journalism. What a shame.

When I reach the main road I suddenly slam to a halt, unable to decide which direction to go. In my panic to reach safety, I have been laboring under the assumption that I would drive straight back to my hotel and lock the deadbolt. But it dawns on me now that my plan may be flawed. There's no guarantee I'd be safe at the hotel. God knows it isn't exactly the fanciest or most secure accommodation I've stayed in. And besides, if I am being followed — and I feel pretty damn confident I am — do I really want to lead them straight to where I'll be sleeping tonight? The thought of those guys hounding me, maybe chaining me up in my own hotel room, is enough to make me gulp.

Hell no. Plan B.

Instead of taking a right, I slam the gas pedal down and spin the wheel to the left, the tires squealing and emitting the sour odor of burnt rubber as I turn the car in the general direction of the coast. I don't know what I'll find there, but some ancient, long-buried memory reminds me that there are usually cops stationed out by the water. By the docks.

I can hardly remember it now, as so much time has passed and I've done such a good job of burying my past self. Thinking of the docks now — it's like looking through a foggy window.

Running up and down the beach, chasing the seagulls and singing old Britney Spears songs from the CD with the flower on it. The memory of the time I scraped my knee on a piece of driftwood and an older neighbor girl scared the hell out of me telling me I was going to get tetanus and die. The sound of my father's voice, buffeted by the coastal breeze, calling out to tell me it was time to go home. That lump in my throat is getting all too familiar. I'm going to have to let myself break down and cry sometime soon.

And a boy… a boy with scraggly dark hair and a charismatic smile. His hands plunging down into the blue depths, grasping for my arms just as my chest goes tight and the world starts to fall into darkness around me. His fingers locking around my wrists, tugging me up out of the churning white foamy water and urging me to *breathe, breathe, it'll be okay, just breathe*. The tickle of sand dragging along my spine, my wet clothes weighing me down. My eyes blinking open and burning with saltwater, focusing hazily on the stormy, purple sky high above me and then closing again just as the boy whispers, "You're safe now."

I'm so far away, so deep in these distant thoughts I have not visited in years, that I have to slam on the brakes to stop the car when it pulls into the nearly-empty parking lot near the entrance to the docks. The sky overhead is getting cloudy and a very light rain starts to drizzle as I catch sight of the police car down the way from me. I hop out of my car and barrel through the rain to tap on the tinted window of the squad car, hoping the cop inside doesn't think I'm some crazed homeless person trying to start something.

I realize now how ridiculous I must look: eyes wide with panic, my whole body woefully overdressed for the occasion and underdressed for the weather, my feet bare and blue except for the holey hosiery. Slowly, the car window rolls down with a faint buzz, to reveal a middle-aged cop with a shaved head giving me a dubious look.

"Anything the matter, ma'am?" he asks flatly.

"Y-yes, sir," I begin, my voice wavering. "I think I'm being followed."

The cop leans out of his window and looks around the empty lot. "By who?"

"Some guys. From… from a warehouse."

At this, the cop's attention flicks back to me instantly, his eyes suddenly full of interest.

"Hold on a sec', miss," he says. He leans away and says something into a receiver, too low and soft for me to catch the words. Then he gets out of the car to stand up in front of me. He's barrel-chested and paunchy, with a bit of a beer gut. He glances down and does a double-take at my lack of shoes before fixing me with a raised eyebrow.

"Where are your shoes?"

"I, um, took them off when I was running." It sounds even stupider out loud.

"You must be freezing. Here, hop in the back," he offers, opening the car door so I can slip inside. I hesitate at first, but then I slide into the seat to get out of the rain.

He shuts the door and stands outside, speaking quietly into the receiver. Over the gentle patter of the rain I can't make out a single word. I hope that he's calling for backup. For several minutes we wait like this, and I surreptitiously take out of my cell phone. It doesn't look to be damaged or anything, but when it hits me that I totally forgot to record any of the scene I witnessed at the warehouse I want to smack myself in the face.

Maybe I'm not cut out for this investigative journalism thing, after all.

Finally, in the distance, I can hear the growl of engines approaching. I strain my eyes to look out the window and make out the approaching shapes of what looks like a fleet of motorcycles. I wrinkle my nose. That's weird. Why would the cop call for backup in the form of moto-cops? Where are they going to put the guys when they arrest them?

But as the bikes get closer my heart sinks. These guys aren't wearing police uniforms. They're dressed in leather jackets and jeans, and they all look mean as hell. *They look like trouble.* They pull into the parking lot quickly and hop off their bikes, dusting off their hands as they walk over to the squad car. My heart is racing in my chest at this point. Where is the backup? Where are the other cops? We can't face these guys without help!

The cop leaning against the car seems unperturbed by the bikers' arrival, standing nonchalantly with his arms crossed on his chest. I want to bang on the window, tell him to take out his gun or something — anything!

What is he doing?!

"Yo! Caught this one. Held her for ya," calls out the cop. I look up at the back of his head through the window, unable to process the words he just said. Caught me? Holding me?

"Get any information out of her?" barks one of the bikers walking up. I realize with a jolt that it's the guy from the warehouse with the blue shirt — the one called Lukas.

"Didn't ask. Just waited for you guys. Like I was told."

"Good work," says another biker. I recognize his voice long before I can make out his face: Leon. The guy in the black shirt who chased me.

The cop is working with these guys. He's a crooked cop. I've been tricked. The realization is coming over me slowly, as it seems just too outlandish to be real. This isn't happening. It can't be. This only goes down in the movies, on true-crime shows.

I'm just some puff-piece journalist from the Big Apple — not an undercover detective.

What if they kill me?

"Whatchu want me to do with her?" asks the cop. In a panic, I slide across the seat to the other side and try to open the door, but there's no way to open it. I've never been in the back of a squad car before, but I'm pretty sure he's got me stuck in here. I pull my legs up to my chest and try to recoil from the scene unfolding outside.

"Just let me talk to her, *khorosho*?" answers Leon.

"I don't want no blood on my seats, eh? You got that?" warns the cop.

"We'll get it detailed for you," sneers Lukas sarcastically.

"Hey man, I'm serious. Chief is on my tail about my unaccounted hours and whatnot. I don't want him gettin' suspicious on me, alright?" complains the officer, holding up his hands.

"Shut up," Leon says, "and open up that door."

"Sure thing, boss."

"No," I murmur softly as the officer pops the door open and Leon reaches inside to grab at me. I slide as far away from him as possible, shaking my head. "No!"

"Come here," Leon growls, grabbing me by the wrists and dragging me out into the rain.

My lungs clinging to that last wisp of oxygen.

"No! Don't hurt me, please!" I cry out, flailing at him.

There's laughter from the biker guys, but Leon doesn't even flinch, pinning me against the slick side of the police car with effortless ease. He leans in close to my face and even in my stark terror I am taken aback by how handsome he is. His eyes are a jade-green, a color surely too vivid to be natural, and there's dark stubble shadowing his strong jaw. His lips are barely parted, his breaths slow and measured, as though he's done this a thousand times. Like this is nothing to him. Like my life is nothing to him.

Even hunched over to get in my face, he towers over me, but I refuse to shrink away — there's nowhere to run now anyway. I am surrounded. There's no way out.

"Who the hell are you?" he asks, his voice so low and deep it sends a thrum through my chest. "Who sent you?"

"Nobody."

"What is your name?"

I close my lips tightly, giving him the fiercest glare I can muster. If I'm going to die in this shitty parking lot, then I am damn sure not going to die cowering like a wimp. It's the least I can do. Be brave, like dad would have wanted. Not give in to the people who very well might have killed him.

Anger flashes in his green eyes and he shakes my shoulders, pressing me harder against the car. "Why were you in that warehouse? What did you see?"

"Why were *you* in that warehouse?" I snap, narrowing my eyes.

There's some unrest among the bikers as they look around at each other, surprised at my brazenness. I gulp.

"None of your damn business," Leon snarls.

"Right back at ya," I reply, surprising even myself. Leon inhales slowly, clearly fighting to hold in his fury at me. One of his hands releases me to swipe back through his dark hair, as he shuts his eyes momentarily. He's losing patience, I can tell. I don't know exactly what that means for me, but it can't be anything good. That's for sure.

"Look," he growls, his voice so low I doubt anyone else can hear him but me, "I don't want to hurt you. But I ask the questions here. Not you."

Well, at least he says he doesn't *want* to hurt me — unlike Lukas behind him, who is rubbing his knuckles and giving me the coldest glare on planet earth. Still, with Leon's hands pinning me like this, his words aren't particularly comforting.

After a long, tense silence, I finally break a little.

"I saw you and that guy behind you," I sigh, gesturing toward Lukas. "You had some other man chained up on the floor in the warehouse. I couldn't really hear what you were saying, though," I lie. It's only half a lie. After all, I did hear some of what they said, but I can't really put it into context at the moment, so it's not especially helpful intel.

"Now we're getting somewhere," Leon says, easing up ever so slightly.

"But I'm not going to tell you why I was there," I add, tilting my face upward defiantly.

"Oh, come on! Just shake the information out of her! We don't have all day!" shouts Lukas, waving his arms angrily. He's definitely the hothead of the crew, that much I can tell.

"Let the man work," drawls the cop, surveying his fingernails as though this is the most routine of activities in the world. And who knows — maybe this *is* everyday fare for him.

"You do realize you're completely surrounded here, right?" Leon prods, raising an eyebrow at my obstinate refusal. "You know you're in the very definition of real and present danger, don't you?"

I nod, still keeping my lips shut tight.

A flicker of something akin to a smile crosses Leon's face, to my surprise. Surely I imagined that. There's no way he's finding any of this amusing.

"Damn, you're one stubborn *devushka,* aren't you?" he murmurs, so softly I barely hear him say it. And there it is: an unmistakable little half-smile. I don't know if it's a good sign, though. I don't know if it means he's going to let me go or if he's just really excited about the prospect of torturing me for information.

"You plan on telling anyone what you saw today?" he persists, his smile giving way to a businesslike, flat expression once again.

I toy with the idea of telling him I'm going straight to the papers with this. But the more practical, self-preserving part of my brain prevails, so I simply shake my head.

And with that, both his arms fall to his side, leaving me free to move. I hesitate, blinking at him in confusion and disbelief. Surely he's not going to just... let me go?

"What are you doing, man?" Lukas exclaims.

Leon rolls his eyes and turns back to him, facing away from me. "Relax, Luke. She doesn't know anything. No point in interrogating an empty witness, *moy brat*."

"You want me to take her in anyway? For trespassing?" asks the cop, barely glancing up.

Leon waves his hand dismissively. "No need."

"Alright," the officer replies. Then he stands up straight and starts yelling, "Okay, okay, disperse the troops. You all have to get outta here before somebody sees you talking to me. You're not the subtlest crowd, you know."

"Embarrassed to be seen with us?" laughs one of the other bikers.

"That hurts our feelings, *sotrudnik,*" cackles another one.

"Yeah, yeah," groans the cop. "Just scram before my chief comes along."

They all start walking back to their respective motorcycles and the cop shoots me a withering glance as he climbs back into the driver's seat of the squad car. "You, too!" he grunts.

"Oh — oh yeah, okay, sorry!" I stammer, hurrying away toward my car. I can't help but feel Leon's green eyes following me as I go. Piercing me straight through.

"Remember what we talked about here today!" he shouts after me.

He doesn't have to add the two words implied to follow…

Or else.

CHAPTER 3 - LEON

I founded the Union Club because us dock workers have to stick together. Because the bosses want to bleed us dry, and the cops want to make it easy for them to do just that. We keep each other safe together, ride together, live together. And if I mean to keep the cops off the backs of the hard-working men and women who keep this rusty chunk of New Jersey running, I've gotta get all of us to work together.

Pushing open the door to The Glass, I step into the smoke-filled bar like it's closer to home for me than my own bed. In a lot of ways, the rough-looking dive next to the drydock really is. It's more than just my bar.

It's *our* bar.

About a dozen heads turn to look me over as I stride across the faded, worn red carpet, and most of them wear the Union Club's patches on their backs. They either raise a hand in greeting or their faces split into a grin as a few voices shout greetings across the bar.

"Hey, Prez!"

"Welcome back, Leon."

"Roy, get our man a beer!"

Even if this weren't where the Union Club went to unwind and talk over how the suits were trying to fuck us over next, I have something of a reputation around town that gets a degree of respect when I walk into places like this. I'm 6'2" of second-generation Russian clad in denim jeans and a worn, dusty leather jacket emblazoned with all the colors of the most well known bunch of men in town. I'm the leader of this pack of hounds, and I look it. My dark hair is shaved on the sides, and the top of it is spiked and sideswept. My cut jaw is covered in stubble, and my pale green eyes demand attention when they lock onto someone else's.

I give a friendly smile back to the rugged bunch of bastards and clasp arms with the giant of a man posted up nearest to the entrance. His face is covered in a large black beard that covers his beaming smile and comes to a rest halfway down his portly body, but I know there's a layer of muscle under all that extra love that could drop a man cold in an instant.

"Missed you today, Genn," my voice rumbles to my old friend, the club's Sergeant at Arms. Gennady Filipov, Genn for short, has been my right-hand-man in the Union Club since I founded it, and I couldn't ask for a better man.

"Heard you had a hell of a weird run-in today, yeah?" he replies as we make our way towards the bar.

The Glass is a safe place to talk business. Probably the safest place in town — it's our base of operations. The first round of Russian immigrants opened this place and called it the Glasnost. Used to be where all the Russian dock workers who could hardly put together a sentence in English met to talk about how things were going.

But all that's our parents' and grandparents' story, and since we all grew up here, it got shortened to The Glass pretty quickly. A few of the older members allowed to wear the club's kutte — jackets covered in our patches — still meet up and swap stories in the mother tongue, but most of us, myself included, only have a trace of a Russian accent in our voices.

We've never stopped talking over the same things, though.

As I make my way into the place, the old familiar faces greet me, each one of them with a story that brought 'em here.

We sidle up to the bar, and my bartender Roy already has a couple of cans out for us. I crack open mine with a nod to him and sit down, leaning back on the bar as I look out around the place.

"We had a run-in with an outsider," I explain as Genn takes a seat beside me, "caught her eavesdropping while me and the boys were finally having a chat with Jack Chandler."

"The old contractor who's started cozying up to the cops?"

I nod with a grimace. "Yeah. I think he's been in their pocket for a while now, and if he has, he'll know what the pigs have been covering up for a long while."

Genn's face started to look more grave, and he took a drink of his beer thoughtfully. "So you're not giving up on running down John LaBeau's murderer, are you?"

I shoot him a look. "Genn, if we let them get it in their heads that the Union Club will allow this kind of shit slide under our watch, they'll walk all over us."

Gen nods thoughtfully. "No doubt. Just sayin' it's a hard search, Prez. Investigators would call it a closed case if they weren't half as crooked as they are around here."

I frown. "Anyway, there's no question she's an outsider. She took off from the warehouse as soon as we saw her, and she ran straight into one of the cops on our payroll."

Genn snorted a laugh. "Maybe she just didn't do her homework."

One of my eyebrows goes up as I try to read Genn's expression. "Homework? So you think she sounds like a fed come to keep an eye on us?"

There's something in Genn's eye that tells me what he's about to say before he even opens his mouth. He lowers his voice as he speaks, even though we're in a bar full of the most loyal men I know. "I dunno about us,

Prez, but you…they might have some old loose ends they're looking to tie up."

I let out a low murmur and take a drink from my beer. As much as I don't want to talk about my past, Genn knows me better than anyone else, and he knows what only a handful of the other patch-members know.

A lifetime ago, my Russian heritage was a lot closer to home. I worked for the Bratva. No, I didn't just work for the Bratva, I killed for them. I was just a kid back then, but I stuck up for the Russian presence around town. The Russian mafia had enemies, and they needed someone who could work swiftly and quietly to do what inevitably needed to be done. It paid well, and the kind of men they had me kill weren't the kind I'd lose a wink of sleep over.

But something got to me. I still don't know what it was, but something in me knew I couldn't keep doing that forever. Some of the more streetwise locals started to know me, started to fear me. I wouldn't build a career with the people I wanted to protect being afraid. This is my home, and these people are my family, not my victims. So I tried to go straight.

Got a job at these very docks a few years back. Wasn't glamorous, but it was honest, and best of all, our union was solid. Where the old times were a long and awful history of making sure us Russians at the docks got shit lives for shit pay, the union let us have a voice together. It gave our little community a heartbeat that spoke loud and strong. We all had fair pay, our jobs were protected, and we worked hard to make sure there was enough to go around for everyone. What had long been a neglected back end of New Jersey was starting to shape up, the community felt stronger, and we were going to provide more jobs for honest, hardworking immigrants and their children.

Then corruption from above came down on us like a hammer, all because we dared try to make a fair living for ourselves. The bosses of the old shipping and drydock companies who'd long held our community in a vicegrip got uneasy. Unions have that effect on the fat-cats that mooch off our hard work. So they worked with the feds, lining their pockets until they could trump up some fake allegations of illegal activity — smuggling, larceny, embezzlement, anything they could get their greasy hands to use against us.

The union bust ruined everything. Our best workers got "laid off," and the old union policies got blamed for it. Men paid by the bosses went around spreading rumors that the union had been smuggling drugs into the community, and incidentally, the cops started turning a blind eye to drug sales from outside the docks to inflate the numbers.

It made my blood boil. Everything we'd worked so hard for was being turned against us. So we did the only thing we could do and banded together, all us dock workers.

So the Union Club was formed, and we've been butting heads with the bosses and their minions to keep them off the honest workers that are left. If they won't allow unions to protect the workers in an official way, we'll protect them outside the law.

But my past with the Bratva has been a liability more often than I like to admit. It wouldn't surprise me in the slightest if someone got a connection from Washington to come investigate me. I can see the headlines now, "Mobster in hiding exposed, affiliated with former corrupt union!" They'll do anything to smear common folk in this town.

"I wouldn't put it past them," I finally answer Genn, "so I want to know who she is, sooner rather than later."

"What's she look like?"

"Hard to miss," I say, and it was true that she'd made a hell of an impression. "Flaming red hair you could spot a mile away. Full lips, high cheekbones, and and a nose that turns up a little at the tip. Blue eyes, bluest eyes I've seen in a long time, bright and keen. Whoever she is, I can tell she's a few notches sharper than most of the cops I've seen. But she didn't identify herself, either — what the fuck kind of game's she playing?" I shake my head. "Anyway, she was dressed like most of the plain-clothed feds are. Trenchcoat and jeans."

The bearded man smiles with a chuckle. "Sounds like you were paying attention, Prez."

I roll my eyes. "Fuck off, Genn." But even as I say it, I can't help but realize he's right. She was fucking hot. I've always been a sucker for a woman who can move like that. And there's something about her that I can't quite place, nagging at the back of my mind like an old dream, but it doesn't come to mind.

Genn nods, understanding, and he turns over to a couple of keen-eyed members wearing the club jackets and playing pool in the corner. "Anya, Vasily! The two of you were patrolling out by the I-78 this morning, you see anyone that sounds like what Prez is looking for?"

Vasily blinks in confusion, but Anya had been listening in on the conversation. The two of them were truck drivers for the docks before the union got busted and the bosses decided they could pay immigrant workers a third of their wages.

"Yeah," said Anya, "I remember someone like that stopping by the same gas station Dmitiri and I were refueling at on her way in. I remember her chatting up the old cashier like they've known each other for years."

"What, are you kiddin' me?" came Rodya's voice from behind the bar, looking over at all of us with a look of disbelief. Rodya's an older guy with a good heart who's lived through the best and worst times, and he'll do just about anything for the club, but he's too laid back to want to earn a kutte. "I'd recognize a gal like that anywhere."

"Got something to say, Rod?" I ask with an arched eyebrow, and Rod laughs at having the upper hand on local intel for once. It's always been a friendly rivalry between the two of us, seeing who can keep the better ear out for the locals: the bartender or the club president.

"W-well yeah! I mean, I'd think you recognize her, wouldn't you?"

I stare at him a moment, then gesture for him to keep talking.

"Shit, Prez," he goes on, "there's only one gal who knows anyone in town who looks like that. You're telling me you really don't remember Cherry?"

The beer can in my hand nearly falls to the ground, and Genn's eyes widen as he slowly looks to me. Hell, half the bar does.

"Cherry," I repeat in disbelief, "Cherry LaBeau."

Out of all I've left behind from my old life, that woman is the one thing I wish I could have back.

"Come on," Rod says with cheerful reminiscence in his voice, "you think I forget anyone who's tried to buy a drink from me underaged? When you and her were teens, I remember you strutting in here all tough, trying to order her a whisky sour. You're the only ones I ever did that for anyway, too, you put on such a good show of it."

Genn bites back a grin, but I chuckle and give him an elbow in the side nonetheless.

Cherry had been someone I knew when I was a teenager around here, it was true. But last I'd heard of Cherry, she'd gone up into the city for bigger and brighter things. Fancy college degree, maybe even a career and a metropolitan apartment. She'd always been the type to want to chase after that.

"Cherry LaBeau," I repeat again, dumbfounded. "Shit, she didn't recognize me either. Have we really changed that much?"

Genn gives a warm smile and claps me on the shoulder. "It's been lifetimes, Prez. Hell, look at me, calling you Prez when I remember you so young you hardly came up past my knee."

I shake my head before downing the rest of my beer and setting it aside.

"Well that tells me something," I say, authority in my voice as I address the rest of the bar. Everyone's already paying attention to me, and I speak to them like the leader I have to be.

"First of all, she's no cop. The Cherry LaBeau I know doesn't deal with cops. At least, unless she's fallen a hell of a long way, and I don't know about you, but I want to find out what the deal is, got it?"

There's a rousing cheer of agreement before the club settles down and I keep talking. "And one more thing — she's got the biggest stake of all in chasing after the truth behind John LaBeau's death," I say, my voice lowering to a normal speaking voice.

"Because John was Cherry's father. And the Union Club never abandons its own."

"Hell no!" comes the general consensus from the bar, the men and women of the club exchanging confident looks and looking to me with admiration. Half of them look ready to go round up some crooked cops right now, but as I open my mouth to speak again, the door of the bar swings open. My vice-prez, Eva, a woman with short, black hair and a sharp nose, strides in with two other patch-members flanking her. Since the union was an equal opportunity employer, so is the Union Club. Unlike most of the other MCs out there, we allow in women as patch members, and it's always worked out in our favor.

"Sorry to break up the party, but we've got trouble," she announces, casting a look around the bar as it quiets down before resting her eyes on me.

"Prez, the FBI is back in town."

CHAPTER 4 - CHERRY

I drive slowly all the way back to town from the coast. Cars pass me every couple of minutes, the drivers glaring back at me like I'm some lunatic for driving under the speed limit. And honestly, any other day I might agree with them. But right now I'm in shock, and I can't bring myself to drive any faster than thirty-five. My hands have a clawlike vice grip on the steering wheel, and I'm holding on so tightly and rigidly that some part of my brain worries I might end up with carpal tunnel or a sprained wrist. I have to remind myself to blink my eyes every now and then, as I stare glassy-eyed at the road in front of me. I've got the Ford rental on cruise control, and my mind is drifting far, far away.

Back to the parking lot miles behind me.

Back to the man with the flashing green eyes and the wicked, damning half-smile.

Something about him awakens a long-buried sentiment deep in my soul, sunken under over a decade of memories. When he grasped my wrists, when he pulled me out of that squad car, I felt a disturbing sense of deja vu. Like he's done it before.

But that's insane. I've never been anywhere near a situation like this before, and I certainly don't know who the guy really is. In fact, all I do know about him is that he's dangerous. He's got some kind of motorcycle group and he's got at least one crooked cop on his side. I also know that he is willing to chain a guy to the filthy floor of an abandoned warehouse — and murder scene — to interrogate him mercilessly.

So, no. I don't think I know him. There's no way.

But then why does he feel familiar?

It's not a conscious recognition. More like a soft, subtle stirring of a strained memory from another lifetime, as though he's stepped into my world from a parallel universe. Like he's an acquaintance of some other Cherry LaBeau, a version of myself I wouldn't recognize today.

I drive the Focus into town, intending to head for the hotel to check in, recuperate and change into some different shoes. But after zoning out for a while, lost in my thoughts, I suddenly realize with a startle that I'm not driving toward the hotel. In fact, I'm on the other side of town entirely, en route to a destination I can find on autopilot, even after all these years.

My dad's old place. My childhood home.

I haven't been back there since my father's death. The funeral was held a few days ago, in a church just outside of town. Even after the service, I returned to my hotel room in Newark, not wanting to commit to a night in Bayonne just yet. It was too close. I couldn't take it.

But today I'm supposed to check into an inn on the west side of town. After all, I didn't leave New York just to hide out in Newark while the mystery of my father's death festers and runs cold in my hometown. I force myself to rip my gaze off the road for a second to check the time. Just after half-past-two. Still early in the afternoon. I suppose since my automatic instincts have guided me back toward home — my old home — I might as well oblige them and go ahead.

Driving down the familiar streets, I'm struck by just how little has changed in the time I've been away. The same mailbox on the hairpin bend is crooked, leaning at a forty-five degree angle like it always has. I swallow back a lump in my throat when I drive past the tall, majestic silver maple in a vacant, overgrown lot I used to climb as a child. Seeing the lacy white undersides of the leaves triggers instant memories in my head, reminding me of how I used to collect the fallen leaves in early autumn into my pockets and dump them into a massive pile in my front yard, poring over the pretty foliage for hours.

When I drive down the road I lived on with my father, I can't stop the tears from burning in my eyes. I don't let them fall just yet, but the urge is definitely building. I haven't cried at all yet. Not even at the funeral. I think the day of the service, I was still in a state of profound shock. Straight off the train from New York City, I was dressed in my sleekest, slinky black dress and a designer blazer. I was in stark contrast to the working-class attendees, my father's friends from the industrial side of town, dressed in shabby suits and well-worn shoes. The older women wore outdated, moth-eaten dresses that probably hadn't seen the light of day since 1995. My professional-grade makeup job made me look like a total fish out of water in comparison to the mostly bare faces filling the pews. Everyone else mourned loudly, unabashedly, unafraid to release their grief and pay their respects, displaying a kind of vulnerability New Yorkers don't dare embrace.

Meanwhile, I sat in the front pew alone, unaccompanied, looking more like a character from a Lifetime movie about a funeral than an actual mourner in real life. I was cordial and responsive to the other funeral-goers when it was required of me, but I didn't say much. I mostly sat quietly and kept to myself until it was over, when I returned to my Newark hotel room.

Even then, alone in my hotel bathtub that night, I did not cry. I wanted to. I tried to. But the tears just sat stubbornly behind my eyes, burning and threatening but never quite spilling free. I suppose I was simply too numb to fully embrace my devastation yet. And then, deciding to visit the warehouse in which he died was more of a whim than anything else. I didn't think it through. I certainly didn't plan it very well.

I realize now, pulling my car into the gravel driveway, that perhaps I was acting recklessly because I didn't have anyone left in the world to tell me not to. My mother disappeared from my life when I was a child, and my father was the only one who ever successfully kept me in line. To be fair, I wasn't a terribly misbehaved little girl — but I have always been obstinate and willful, causing some trouble for my teachers and babysitters growing up. But my dad… my dear, patient, honest father, all he ever had to do was give me a disappointed look and I immediately shaped up. He never raised his voice or lifted a hand in anger, never did anything to clip my wings or tether me down to earth.

He simply loved me, so deeply and unconditionally, that I could not bear the thought of disappointing or hurting him. It was the way I wanted to raise my own children someday. *A very distant someday*, I think sadly, as I have never even had a serious relationship that lasted more than six or seven months. I was a serial dater, not a serious dater.

Every man I meet seems to want to tie me down and keep me from flying away, even if at first they pretend to be fine with my career ambitions. I suppose my image and reputation precedes me and damns me in this regard. Cherry LaBeau the puff-piece writer doesn't have big dreams beyond attending New York Fashion Week and landing a Tiffany diamond someday. But the real Cherry LaBeau — the real me that nobody sees reflected in my flimsy, gossipy published pieces — wants something more meaningful, more *real*. When it comes down to it, when the ditzy pretty-girl image is ripped away, no man ever wants to stick around.

But I know my father would never want his only daughter to be anyone's trophy wife. He wanted so much more for me, and he believed in me when nobody else did. I just need to find a guy who will have my back, who can keep up with me.

Someone strong and commanding, but mischievous and adventurous…

Instantly and inexplicably, Leon pops into my head. Sitting in the front seat of my car, idling in the driveway of my late father's house, I snort out loud. What is wrong with me? Is there a "temporary insanity" step to the phases of grief I don't know about? Why the hell am I fantasizing about a guy who chased me for miles and pinned me to a crooked cop's car and threatened my life? I watched him torture a guy chained to a warehouse floor, for God's sake! Obviously my father's death is sending me into some kind of bizarre crazy-person spiral.

Morbidly, I hesitate over the ignition, almost afraid to cut the engine. As long as I'm idling, it's like I'm not really here. Like this is all a bad dream, and I'm going to wake up any moment now. Biting my lip, I close my eyes and turn the key. The gentle vibrations of the engine cut out, leaving me in the still silence of a dead man's driveway.

I don't know why I'm here, but I tell myself that it's to gather more information about how my dad might have died. I convince myself that there's a good reason for me to get out of my car, climb the front steps to the screened-in porch, and fumble for the key in my pocket. The house was left to me, along with everything else my dad had to his name. Which wasn't much.

I unlock the door and walk into the front foyer, glancing around. The electricity and air conditioning are still running, as his death is so recent. Everything looks pretty much the same way it always did. The house is only about 1,400 square feet, with two bedrooms and one cramped little bathroom. The living room coffee table is covered in papers. I cock my head at this odd sight; my father was always shockingly neat and organized. He never left documents just lying around, whether they were important or not. I wonder, with a pang of guilt, if maybe he just got a little messier over the years, without me around to help out. Not that he was even that old when he passed. He and my mother got together in their teens — they were highschool sweethearts. My parents were only in their early twenties when I was born, so my dad was just shy of his forty-eighth birthday when he died.

It hits me now, again, just how strange his death is. He wasn't even fifty yet. What kind of physically active, religiously healthy forty-seven-year-old just drops dead out of nowhere? Sure, the police told me it was an industrial accident — that he was simply killed doing the same kind of thing he did every day of his life for over twenty years. A freak incident. A moment's slip. A little mistake with a massive cost. Simply in the right place at the wrong time.

I knew, though, that something wasn't right about it. That there's no way this was an accident. And in school, they always told me to trust my gut. That it would lead to the truth.

"He was a hardworking, honest man right down to the very last," one of his coworkers told me at the funeral, clasping my hand in both of his. There were tears shining in his eyes, a frown on his weathered face. I vaguely recalled him from my childhood as one of my dad's friends — a man named Chuck, I think. His wife used to bring over casseroles on Sundays every once in awhile. I remember they tasted like salt and sawdust, but she was so sweet that we ate the whole thing every damn time anyway.

I sit down on the sunken-in, decades-old couch and tuck my curly red hair behind my ear to look over the papers on the coffee table. I can't resist. And this makes me feel like I'm doing something, like I've got a reason to be here snooping around. It's *business*.

I scoop up a stack of papers and lean back on the couch to look them over, only to hear a strange crinkling noise from underneath me. I wriggle to the side and reach inside the cushions, my fingertips coming in contact with what feels like more papers. But smoother. Slick. Glossy.

Photographs.

I extract them and look through them with a dubious expression. They're pictures of equipment from his workplace, with names, dates, and notes scribbled on the back. The documents look like health code violation notices, employee complaints, and some handwritten letters. Some of them are in my father's signature left-handed scrawl, while others I don't recognize at all.

"What the hell was he doing with all this?" I mumble aloud, shaking my head.

Just then, I hear a strange rumble from outside. I look up in confusion, thinking at first that someone must have pulled into the driveway. But then I realize it's the combined sounds of several smaller, louder engines. My heart stops for a moment and I jump to my feet, the papers and photographs falling in disarray on the floor.

Motorcycles.

CHAPTER 5 - LEON

"Mickey Lamar," I say as I pace around the bar, addressing the gathered men and women. "We owe that son of a bitch a visit. For those of you just getting here, yeah, you heard right," I state firmly, looking each and every one of them in the eye as I come to a stop in the center of the room, arms crossed. "The FBI is back in town. Eva says intel is still shaky, but if I know the FBI, they've sent Doyle and his boys down after us again."

There's a general murmur around the bar, and I can tell that some of the newer blood look uneasy, while most of the older patch-members have knit their brows and wear bitter grimaces. Us veterans have sour memories about Agent Charles Doyle and the FBI in general, and I suspect there've been rumors trickle down over the years.

That makes today's visit to Mickey all the more important. A morale booster.

"Alright, none of you get any assumptions in your heads, alright? Stick together and keep your nose out of the dirt, and whatever happens, never talk to any cops if you don't know where their paycheck is coming from. Got it?"

There's a shout of agreement from the club, and I give a curt nod.

"Good. Now who knows about this fucker Mickey?"

Lukas, our treasurer, speaks up first. "That the guy who owns Mickey's North Liquors?"

"You got it," I say, cracking my knuckles. "Mickey's an older guy, been running that shithole of his for decades. Never met an employee who's come out of there without getting burned bad. There've been rumors about this bastard getting away with anything with his employees. Seventy-hour work weeks, no overtime, weaseling his way out of sick leave. Word through the grapevine at the unemployment office is that Mickey just laid off two of his workers with no notice, no severance, and no prospects. Incidentally, one of 'em just found out she's pregnant."

There's a chorus of outraged shouts from the club.

"Piece of shit!"

"Typical, fuckin' fat-cats."

I wave my hand at all of them to get them to settle down. "Alright, alright. Let's take that enthusiasm where it matters, alright? Now I don't know about you, but I think Mickey pulling this shit is a little too well timed to be a coincidence. Are we gonna let the FBI be what sends us running when the worker folks need us?"

There's a shout to the effect of "Fuck no!"

"I didn't think so," I say, striding towards the door. "Now let's ride."

Minutes later, the wind whips across my face as our bikes tear through the streets of the city, our line of roaring engines announcing us as we made our way to the outskirts of town, a good ways from The Glass.

The FBI may be in town, but I won't let that get in the way of business. After all, how can the workers of the city feel protected if we take to the hills the second the suits from Washington show up? The people need someone who will do what needs to be done through thick and thin.

It doesn't take us long to get to the liquor store. There aren't many customers around at this time of day, but it's getting later, and the after-work crowd will roll through before long.

I don't mind that. It won't take long to get our message across to Mickey.

Our bikes take up most of the run-down parking lot. It's a shoddy looking place with a burned-out letter in the grungy sign. Mickey cuts corners wherever he can, either in the employee's paychecks or the building's upkeep.

I stride up to the building and see a young man, presumably an employee refilling an ice machine out front. He glances up at me as I approach, then does a double-take as he notices the rest of the club behind me, looking alarmed.

"C-can I help you?" says the man in a thickly accented voice.

"I don't know," I say, "you a new hire here?"

"Hire? Uh, yes sir."

"How much is the old man paying you?"

The man is visibly shaking now, and the fear in his eyes tells me everything I need to know even before he begins shaking his head and feigning not being able to understand my question. He's clearly an immigrant being paid under the table.

"The answer is 'not fairly,'" I say to him, giving the terrified man a pat on the back as I nod for the rest of the club to follow me inside. Some of the boys give him an encouraging nod as they file in after me, but the man is too terrified to react.

As we slowly flood the entrance to the shady liquor store, Mickey Lamar himself raises his head from behind the counter, a perpetual scowl on his face. He's a wiry guy in his fifties, thin from doing nothing but working the shop his whole life and blessed with a kindly, elderly face. But the moment his eyes fall on all of us, his whiskery face blanches behind his thick-framed glasses.

"Fucking shit," I hear him whisper as he starts to fumble at the counter, but before he can do anything, I hold out a hand to him while the other goes instinctively to the pistol tucked in my back.

"Hold up there, Mickey," I say as I circle around the counter before tilting my head towards the club. "Fellas, mind tellin' Mickey's treasured customers that he'll be closing shop early today?"

The club obliges, and the few customers in the shop are politely asked to make their way out while Mickey and I glare each other down over the counter. My hand is still at my gun. I don't think Mickey has it in him to try anything stupid, but I know there's a shotgun behind that counter, and I'm not taking any chances.

"What the fuck do you thugs want, barging into my store like this? I'm an honest man, I pay my taxes! Isn't that what you jobless fucks tout about defending all the time? Get the fuck out of here!"

"Come on, Mickey," I say, the world's fakest smile on my face. "We haven't paid a visit in a long time, and that's how you're gonna say 'hello'? We just thought we'd stop in and check in with you and your valued employees since we've got nothing else to do today, isn't that right, Eva?"

"That's right," my Vice concurs, "I hear one of them has a bun in the oven, is that right? Thought we'd congratulate the expectant mother."

"Funny thing is, Mickey," I say, "I didn't see her on the way in, but I did see a new face at the ice machine. His English isn't too good, but I'm sure you're helping him out with that, aren't you? After all, everyone knows you're a generous kinda guy."

The look in Mickey's eyes is positively glowing with fire.

"Alright alright, get off my ass, shithead," he snarls. "I know what the fuck this is about, so cut the bullshit."

"You want *me* to cut the bullshit?" I laugh while some of the club checks through the bottles on the shelves idly, but I know it's a ruse—their eyes are watching the entrance and the employee doors for signs of trouble.

"That's rich, Mickey, real rich. Alright, so if you wanna cut the bullshit, let's cut the bullshit." I step towards the counter, taking my hand off my gun and resting both palms on the surface in front of me, my face about a foot away from Mickey's scowl.

"Why don't you explain to me why, the second the suits from Washington start cropping up in town, you think your ass can get away with firing a couple of honest employees and hiring a couple of immigrants you pay a third of a living wage in their place? Why don't you start with that, huh?"

"I ain't gotta say shit to any of you Russkys."

There's a quiet confidence in his eyes, like a smug, petulant child who knows he has the teacher on his side in the middle of a playground scrap. I know it's because he feels safe with the FBI around town. And I know that to some degree, he's right in that security. One fed happens to be driving by the shop right about now, and we'd all be in the slammer before sundown.

But I'm not going to let that threat stop me. Not when there are folks' livelihoods at stake.

"Look, Mickey," I say, my voice becoming deadly serious, "let me put it this way. Now, I know you think you've got your ass covered with the big boys from out of state coming around town to clean out thugs like us, but it isn't gonna work that way. Unless you like the idea of having trouble with the club," I give a sharp nod towards me crew, "then you're gonna give those two employees you just laid off their jobs back. And they're gonna have the exact same pay as they had when your slimy ass kicked them out."

"Boss?" comes the voice of one of my men, but I'm focused on Mickey.

Mickey starts laughing as though I've just played right into his hand.

"That so? Well, sure, I won't mind doing that, so long as you go tell those hardworking immigrants outside I've gotta fire them 'cause the local gang doesn't like anyone hiring outsiders."

That pushes the wrong buttons for me. Faster than Mickey can get another word out, my hand flashes forward and snatches him by the collar, pulling him close as he gasps in surprise. Guess the old fart didn't think we'd so much as touch him. I don't even hear one of my men call my name again from near the door.

"Oh no, you sniveling little shit," I snarl at him, "things are gonna change for them, too, but for the better. Not only are you going to keep them on, but you're going to pay them a fair wage, too. Not a cent less than what you hired the other two employees at. Think you're going to get away with cutting corners at poor workers' expense? Fuck that. You're about to become the most generous man in the neighborhood, Mickey."

"And just what the fuck do you think you're gonna do about it, you potato-eating good-for-nothing?"

His voice is unwavering, but with our face so close, I can see the glint of doubt in his eyes. He's starting to doubt that the threat of the FBI will keep things from getting real, and fast. My fist clenched, and I open my mouth to retort.

"PREZ," Eva shouts at me, and this time I turn to look at her just as the door to the liquor store swings open.

Standing there at the entrance of the store is Cherry, mouth agape as she pushes past my man posted at the door and looks me dead in the eye as my fist is raised toward Mickey.

CHAPTER 6 - CHERRY

"What the hell is this?" I exclaim, looking around the liquor store with my mouth agape.

After hearing the motorcycles rumble by earlier, I couldn't resist the urge to follow them. Even though I knew I should be cautious, something told me I needed to find out where they were going. I followed them in my rental car, keeping about a block behind just in case they decided to look back and recognize my Focus. I was confused when I saw them pull into the parking lot of the liquor store which has been here ever since I can remember.

Mickey's is where my dad used to stop on the way home from a long day at work to pick up a six-pack for himself, and a soda for me. It has memories, but they're all innocuous. So I had no idea what the biker gang could possibly want with the store, besides just buying alcohol to fuel whatever criminal activities they were getting into tonight.

At first, I sat in my car in the parking lot, biting my lip nervously, trying to talk myself into just driving back to my hotel and pretending none of today happened. But when all the biker guys disappeared into the store and stayed inside for longer than an average trip to the liquor store should take, that same sense of duty and fate urged me to look into it.

So here I am now, standing in the midst of what looks like some kind of shakedown. Various motorcycle guys and even a couple women I didn't notice before are stationed throughout the little liquor store. In any other situation, their arrangement might just look like a bunch of people who just happen to be browsing the shelves at the same time. But with my heightened awareness of the tension in the air, it is apparent to me that they're strategically spread out to cover the store.

And Leon is here, with his fist raised in a combative stance, looking like he's just about to rip into some wiry, fifty-something guy in a shabby business suit. The guy looks vaguely familiar, and it dawns on me that I saw him around the store on the few occasions when my dad stopped off here and left me sitting in the truck. I think it's Mickey, himself. The guy the store's named after.

In the next few seconds, a million little things seem to happen in slow motion. The man I shoved past at the doorway comes up behind me, his footsteps heavy and quick. Leon has turned to look back at me, his green eyes going wide with alarm and confusion.

A woman's voice somewhere to my left cries, "Watch out!"

And then my eyes flick back instinctively to Mickey, who has used Leon's moment of distraction to quickly draw out something small, black, and shiny.

A gun.

"Don't tell me how to run my damn business!" Mickey shouts, a wicked grin on his face as he lowers the gun to point toward Leon's chest. My whole body goes hot and cold with fear. Instantaneously, several biker guys come barreling down the aisles of liquor, bottles shattering to the floor left and right. One of the guys closest to the showdown between Mickey and Leon dives for the store owner, his thick, tree-trunk arms wrapping around Mickey's legs as the two of them fall to the floor in a heap.

On the way down, there's a deafening crack as the gun goes off. I can *feel* the bullet whiz past me, and then there's the sound of more glass breaking as the bullet goes through the window. The next sound I hear is the worst one yet: an agonized scream in a foreign language.

Someone's been shot.

"You fucking *mudak*!" Leon bellows, kicking Mickey hard in the side as he lies crumpled on the ground, pinned under the bearded biker guy's powerful arms.

"I'm sorry, Prez," grunts the biker, shaking his head and looking up at Leon dolefully. "I didn't know the gun was gonna go off. *Chert voz'mi*, I tried to stop him — "

"Not your fault, Genn," Leon replies, "Just keep him down."

"Oh my God," I murmur, turning around to see a woman in a leather jacket bolt out the entrance and kneel down beside a fallen guy outside. Through the shattered window I can make out the spread of scarlet blood pooling on the pavement.

"B-blood," I mumble, just as my head starts to get fuzzy inside. I don't do well with blood. Not at all. They make me lie down on a stretcher any time I have to give blood because I have a reputation for fainting. I start to feel that familiar, terrible wave of nausea and lightheadedness.

"Man down!" shouts the woman from outside, looking up through the hole in the window to give Leon a panicked expression.

"Where's he hit?" asks a guy running past me.

"Left shoulder blade. Anya, we need you!" answers the woman. Another female biker comes bolting past, her cropped blonde ponytail bouncing. She nearly shoves me out of the way in her haste to get outside. She crouches down next to the guy on the ground and immediately rips his shirt to make a tourniquet from the thin material.

"Oh my… oh no," I mumble, my vision going dark.

Some guy, possibly the huge bearded biker named Genn, calls out, "Uh oh, think we got a fainter there, Prez."

I can feel my knees buckling beneath me but before I start to fall, a pair of muscular arms catch me around the chest and hold me up. "Already got one down, can't afford another," growls Leon in my ear, sending a shiver down my spine.

"What is going on?" I ask, my voice wavering and weak.

"I don't know — you tell me," he retorts, spinning me around slowly to face him. Once again, his hands are on my shoulders, bracing me. This is the second time in one day.

In my hazy brain, the only words I can manage are: "We gotta stop meeting like this."

Leon sighs and pats my cheek, trying to break me out of my near-faint.

"Gotta get this guy back to church, immediately," calls out a woman.

Leon looks past me to give her a nod. "Alright, do your best. Eva! Rod! Get our patient up off the ground and get him out of here so Anya can stitch him up. Everybody out! I'll meet you back at church later, *khorosho*?"

"Got it, Prez."

"Byet ostorozhen!"

With that, every single one of the bikers file out of the liquor store at once, except for Leon and the bearded, bear-like guy pinning Mickey to the floor. Leon looks back over his shoulder at the two of them, and the bearish guy speaks up.

"What should I do with him?"

"Stand him up, Genn. We're gonna have a little business chat."

"You think you got time for that?" spits Mickey as Genn swings him up onto his feet effortlessly. "Nosy neighbors 'round this neighborhood must've called the cops by now. This gun, ya know, it's small but it's still awfully loud."

"Yeah, and I bet you had the good sense to register it under your name legally, eh?" Leon says, turning back away from me to take an aggressive step toward Mickey, who shrinks back.

Mickey is silent.

"That's what I thought. They're gonna get here and see that gun and know exactly who shot it. You wanna go down for shooting an innocent man, Mr. Lamar?"

"Pfft!" the store owner snorts. "He's an illegal. They'll just toss his ass back over the border and be done with it. I'll just tell 'em he lunged at me or something. Self-defense is still a valid reason to fire in this country. And besides, who're the cops gonna believe: me or some foreigner with no ID?"

Leon gives Genn just the slightest, subtlest nod. The bearlike guy pulls back and pummels Mickey in the gut, hard, causing him to gasp in pain and shock. With the wind knocked out of him so suddenly, he doubles over.

"Here's what's gonna happen," Leon says, calmly and quietly. "You're gonna hire back everyone you let go, including the innocent man you just wounded, once his shoulder's all healed up. And speaking of which, you are also going to pay for every dime of his medical care until he's even better off than when he first met your slimy ass."

"Or what?" Mickey manages to choke out, though his arms are wrapped around his stomach like he's trying not to wince.

"Well, we don't exactly have a contract drawn up, but I think you'll find that Genn here can be very convincing. I think he's all the incentive you'll need."

Genn knees Mickey in the back and the store owner yelps in pain.

"Go to hell," he groans viciously.

"Fine, we'll throw in another benefit. We'll get rid of the gun."

"You mean you'll confiscate it," Mickey snaps.

"Look, do you really wanna have that gun in your hands when the cops show up? Illegal alien or not, it's gonna look real incriminating already that a man *you* hired got shot on *your* property with *your* gun while *you* were on the premises. Don't you think? And take in the fact that he's not from around here — well, that jury is gonna take one look at your racist, good-for-nothing face and convict you before you can even take a breath, Mr. Lamar."

"So why not let us take that smoking gun off your hands since you obviously don't know how to handle it anyway?" Genn adds, looking to Leon for approval.

Mickey is fuming, shaking his head at the floor.

"Agreed?" Leon prompts, bending down to stare at Mickey, who's all but kneeling on the floor in front of him by this point.

In response, Mickey simply drops the gun on the floor. Leon snatches it up and latches the safety back on before tucking it into his leather jacket. "Good choice. Nice doing business with you, Mr. Lamar."

"Genn, get him into the back room and leave him there. Then get outta here while you still can," Leon orders. "I've gotta talk to Miss LaBeau."

At the sound of my name, I freeze up. How did he figure out who I am? Did he look me up? Was he watching me? Was he only pretending not to know me when he questioned me this morning? Then he looks back at me. As soon as those vivid mossy-green eyes land on me, my whole body tingles with a low thrum of electricity. He's a lightning bolt of a man, and I find myself oddly exhilarated at the idea of being left alone with him here.

At yet another crime scene. I can't help but wonder which one of us is attracting such dangerous situations: him? Or me?

Genn replies curtly, "You got it, Prez." He drags Mickey off down the aisles, the two of them stepping all over broken glass and puddles of spilled booze as they go. Mickey is kicking and screaming like a petulant toddler, but Genn restrains him easily, without even having to say a word or break a sweat. He locks the store owner in the storage room at the back before jogging out an emergency exit door on the side of the building. I hear the rumble of his motorcycle engine firing up, the roar fading away to nothing as Genn disappears down the road.

Leaving me all alone in this fucked-up scene with Leon.

He's looking at me almost warily, like he doesn't know how to approach me. I wonder if he knows more about me than I know about him — he's got to, since what I know about him is hardly anything at all. I take in his enormous height, his muscular build, his jet-dark hair and those damning, electric green eyes.

I swallow hard. He seems to notice this — the tiniest but tell-tale sign that I'm afraid. That he has the upper hand here. After all, he's the one with the gun tucked into his jacket.

"Why are you here?" he asks in that deep, commanding voice.

"I — I think we should both just go," I breathe. "Cops will be here soon."

"A call to this neighborhood?" he scoffs bitterly. "They'll take their damn time."

"Please just let me leave. I'll go home. I'll stay out of this — whatever this is," I plead.

Leon steps closer and shakes his head. I instinctively fall back slightly, even though some foolish, inexplicable part of me longed to get closer to him. Much closer. I forced that little voice in my mind to pipe down.

"You're in it now, *prekrasnyy*. No going back," he replies quietly.

"I didn't mean to intrude. I messed up. I should never have — "

"Ah, but you did," he croons, moving in on me. "You wanna play cops and robbers? Well, you got what you came looking for. Hope it lives up to your expectations."

I shake my head quickly, putting my hands up in front of me in surrender. "No, no, I swear I'll just disappear and you'll never see me again. I promise."

He reaches out with lightning-quick speed and grabs hold of my wrists. He's so close now I can feel the heat radiating off of his hard body. Those jade-green eyes search my face earnestly, as though he's trying to glimpse my soul. Like he's trying to remember something he once lost, something far away and out of reach.

"I won't let that happen," he answers quietly. "Not again, Cherry."

There it is again, that burning warmth that passes down the entire column of my body at the sound of his strong, baritone voice saying my name. My flimsy, silly name.

"How do you know my name?" I dare to ask, regarding him fearfully.

Leon's eyes flash dark momentarily, as though I've offended him. No, softer than that. Like I've hurt his feelings or something. But surely a man like this doesn't get his feelings hurt very easily? Besides, what could I possibly have done to him?

"You don't remember me at all, do you?" he asks, a little sadly.

Sunlight dappled through gem-blue water. Wondering if this is the last thing I'll see as my chest grows tight, the sharp pain in my lungs threatening to drag me into unconsciousness as the oxygen in my brain dissipates into nothing.

Hands around my wrists. Just like now. Holding me up, up out of the water.

I gasp at the realization. "I… I remember you," I whisper, scarcely able to believe it.

"The girl from the shore," he says, almost fondly. His thumb traces a soothing circle over my hand as he opens his mouth to say something else.

Just then, there is the distant wail of police sirens, jolting us from our shared reverie. The cops are coming. Panic floods into my veins and I tense up. Leon takes my hand and pulls me along behind him. "We've got to go!"

"Where are we going?"

"I'll know when we get there!" he calls back over his shoulder. We run out the door and across the parking lot. There's only one helmet hanging off the handlebars of his motorcycle, and he tosses it to me, eschewing his own safety to ensure mine. "Hop on!" he orders.

Before I can think better of it, before I can ask what will become of my rental car, before I can talk myself out of it, I do exactly as he says. I climb onto the motorcycle behind him, clinging to his hard chest as we peel out onto the road in the opposite direction of the police sirens.

CHAPTER 7 - LEON

My bike feels unfamiliar with the weight of someone else on it. I live on my bike more than I do on my own two feet, more often than not, and my bike feels comfortable enough under me that it's like just another appendage. So having someone hanging on behind me feels as unusual as a new arm.

"Where are we going?" I hear Cherry shout from behind me as I tear through the streets, but I don't bother trying to answer. The wind would just take the words from me, if she isn't used to talking on a bike.

Instead, I just nod to the alley I'm about to turn down, and I pull her hands a little tighter around my waist before taking a sharp turn around a corner.

I have to be quick. The local police are probably the only ones who know the back alleys of Bayonne as well as we do, and I don't know which officers are tailing me. For all I know, it could be some rookie too new to town to know not to answer this call, or it could be a couple of seasoned veterans with an FBI agent right behind them. The wake of a shooting isn't the time to take those kinds of chances.

Mickey's isn't far from the worse-off parts of town, but as I take us through the back alleys and narrow side-streets that make up the older parts of Bayonne, things get a little rougher pretty quickly. We pass by yards with run-down cars in them, a few of them with cinderblocks holding them up where the tires should be. There's an old American flag waving on tarnished flagpoles over a house with a couple of boarded-up windows. There's a family with at least ten children holding what looks like a little quinceañera outside, the father wearing tattered overalls and the mother with a tired look on her face as she herds the group around.

This is where most of the workers live, and I know it's thoroughly our territory. The sooner we can find somewhere to hide out in a place like this, the easier it will be for the two of us to utterly vanish. As we pass by, some of the locals who happen to be in their front yard give us friendly greetings. A young man with arms stained black from working at a repair shop gives us a smile and a wave while he gets his mail as I drive by, and I nod back. An older guy with a limp who I recognize as a local school bus driver does the same as he gets out of his vehicle, just now off work.

A middle-aged woman tending her garden down the road notices us approaching, and she makes her way to the sidewalk and flags us down. I recognize her as one of the workers from the factory a few blocks off the docks; she and her wife have shared a drink with the club more than a few times.

"What's goin' on?" she says by way of greeting, giving both of us a curt nod. "Everything alright? Got a new face with you, Prez." She's not a club member, but it's become kind of a town nickname for me. A few people have talked about making me president of the union when we get things back together, but for the time being, I know it's just a term of endearment.

"Need a place to lay low," I say, and she gives another sharp nod.

"Say no more. Loretta's sick inside, otherwise I'd let you crash here, but the Lawrences across the street look like they've got doors open to ya."

I turn my head, and I see the face of the elderly Gerald Lawrence poking out the door of the old brownstone. A smile and give him a nod before turning back to the woman. "'Preciate it, Jan."

"Is everyone in town this friendly?" Cherry asks from behind me. Jan laughs back.

"For Prez, yeah. Union boys have given us more of a leg up than all the cops in town put together, chickadee. You're in good hands."

Before Cherry can reply, I turn the bike towards the brownstone and pull around the residence, carefully moving my bike around the back where it'll be at least partially out of sight. In the little strip of land that makes for a backyard, Wanda Lawrence steps out from the backdoor, leaning on her cane and giving us both a loving smile.

"Well look who it is, long time no see, Leon! Come on in, come on in, Gerald says you'd like a place to rest while things settle down outside."

"Much obliged, Mrs. Lawrence," I say gratefully while I help Cherry off the bike.

"Are they alright? Are you sure this is safe?" Cherry whispers to me after she takes her helmet off and shakes out her hair. I give her a boyish grin back, unable to keep myself from appreciating how good she looks.

"Relax. These two go way back with me. This is a safe place to lay low for a few hours while the cops buzz off."

Cherry looks uncertain, but she nods, following me up to the door as Wanda holds it open for us, smiling warmly as we step into the quaint little kitchen. Gerald is standing inside, still casting glances at the front window as he makes his way to the kitchen to give my hand a firm shake.

"Thanks for this," Cherry says, venturing to break the ice with what were total strangers to her. "We really appreciate it."

Gerald lets out a hearty laugh. "Oh, you must be new around town — Leon here has more than earned a place here any time. When Wanda had her fall last year, his boys made sure groceries got here every week while I had to run the shop."

"Not like Anya wouldn't have done it herself if we didn't know about it," I answer with a chuckle, and Gerald nods, a hint of sadness still in his eyes at the mention of the name.

"Why don't you two get settled in the living room while we make you all some coffee?" Wanda offers, and I give her a nod.

"Thanks, ma'am." I lead Cherry to the cramped living room, covered in old, musty furniture, the walls invisible under all the pictures of the cute old couple's family and life together. It's a quaint little place.

Cherry takes a seat on one of the armchairs across from me. I can tell she looks more than a little uncomfortable, and I can't really blame her. It's been a hell of a day for her, to put it lightly.

As the owners head back into the kitchen to give us some privacy, Cherry finally looks me in the eye, chewing her lip a moment before speaking.

"What happened to this place, Leon?"

There it is. The question I knew would be coming from the moment I knew it was Cherry come back to town.

"That's a big question, Cherry," I say with a sigh. "Where do you want me to start?"

Cherry seems at a loss for a moment, but then just gestures vaguely outside. "I mean, all *this*. My school bus dropped kids off in this neighborhood when we were in high school. It wasn't anything like this back then. I remember green grass and pretty decent houses. I know you see things differently when you're a kid, but…"

"Things went downhill pretty fast while you were gone," I say, and the memory of those old times takes me back to a place I hadn't thought of for a long while. Cherry was having that effect on me in more ways than one, I was starting to realize. "I know your dad didn't see eye-to-eye with what those of us in the union were doing during the strike, but once the bosses broke us up, it was easy for them to start driving this town into the dirt. Wages dropped, people spent less and worked more, and the only people who kept their pockets lined were the goons up top."

I can tell Cherry looks a little skeptical. Part of that is her instinct to question, I know. She's always had that kind of spark to her, came from her father. But I know she probably has a different predisposition to this place than us locals do.

"So what, the union dies and poverty just kind of...happens? I know everyone seems to like you pretty well around here, Leon, but I mean, how bad can they make it? Dad wasn't big on the unions, and he seemed to do fine after the bust."

"Lotta the folks who didn't side with the union came out alright in the aftermath," I agree with a nod, "but he took a pay cut just like everyone else. You don't remember him working later nights for the time before you left?"

Cherry furrows her brow, and the pieces begin to fall together in her mind. "He said he was putting aside cash for a college fund when he started moonlighting."

"A lot of people had to start 'saving for a special occasion' after the bust," I say, a grim smile on my face. "I know your dad didn't always love what we did, Cherry, but those of us the bosses decided to strike back at felt it hard. Nowadays, this club is the only thing keeping the place together. It's not like it's ideal, but until they listen to our demands, it's what we're forced to do to survive."

Cherry looks like she's starting to understand, but to drive things home, I nod my head up to one of the pictures on the wall.

It shows a young man and a woman who looks like she's got as much Russian in her as all the rest of the immigrants.

"See that? The guy in that photo is Henry Lawrence — Gerald and Wanda's son. He was one of ours."

"I didn't see him at the liquor store," Cherry says.

"No, but the lady, Anya, pushed past you there," I point out, and I see recognition in Cherry's face. "The two of them got hitched a few years back. Real happy couple, both of 'em." I smile, remembering the wedding party the two of them had, and it seemed like a lifetime ago.

"The cops brought Henry in a few years ago as a suspect in a robbery. Claimed he was an accomplice of a couple of strangers from out of town who hit a convenience store off the interstate. He just happened to be patrolling in the area, and they took him in." I pause, my lips tight for a moment. "He died while the police had him. Official story was he was resisting, tried to jump the cops in transit. Everyone who knows Henry knew he couldn't hurt a fly, but those fuckers…"

Cherry is paying rapt attention, and I lean forward, clasping my hands together.

"Anya was inconsolable for the longest time. She was a nurse back then, but after Henry died, she took his place in the club. Still rides his bike and wears his kutte to this day. Nowadays, she's our medic. She'll be making sure those workers back at the liquor store are well taken care of on their way to the hospital. I wouldn't put it above the cops around here to try and make sure they don't pull through so they can't testify to anything in court. As if most of the judges aren't bought."

Cherry is quiet for a long time, a thoughtful expression on her features. As I watch her, I realize that while I've grown so hard over the years, developed such a thick skin to resist all the constant repression the people of the town face while just trying to scrape by... Cherry hasn't lost one iota of the youthful energy she had the day she left. She's as vigorous as she is gorgeous, like a bolt of lightning trying to surge through her old hometown and hitting resistance she wasn't expecting to find.

I have to admit, jaded as I am, it's a little inspiring to see. A lot inspiring, actually.

"To say Dad didn't approve of what you all were doing is putting it lightly," Cherry says with a small smile. "Especially after the name 'Union Club' started cropping up."

"He always was a straight arrow," I say with a laugh, shaking my head. "And to be honest, I don't blame him. It's a scary thing to see an MC crop up in your front yard, I can understand that."

"These people really seem to value you, though," Cherry admits, glancing back to the kitchen, where the smell of fresh coffee has started to waft from. "Hell, maybe…" she pauses, obviously uncomfortable getting her thought out. She opens her mouth to continue, and I suspect I know what she's going to say, but she lets the words die in her mouth as Wanda comes shuffling into the room with a broad smile on her face.

"Here we are. I hope neither of you wanted decaf."

"Thanks," I say with a smile, taking the coffee and feeling invigorated by the smell alone as Wanda hands Cherry her mug.

"Now let me tell you, dearie," Wanda tells Cherry with a grandmotherly smile, "I don't know how long you've been in town, but if you're riding with Leon here, why, you couldn't be in better hands."

"It sounds like it," Cherry says with a nervous laugh. I can't help but grin. She seems a little uncomfortable around older people. I forget that living in a city like she has can let you stick to your own age group pretty exclusively.

She and Wanda exchange some brief small-talk about where she's from and where she's lived, and while she does, I find myself surprised by an old, familiar feeling in my chest.

I only knew Cherry for the shortest of times when she was in town, sure. But seeing her again has been like seeing the ghost of an old friend. Maybe she just reminds me of the life I used to see in Bayonne, before the bosses had a chance to really dig their claws in. But the more I watch her mannerisms, the way she unconsciously plays with a lock of her hair, the way she talks...I don't know. I feel like I'm talking to an old sweetheart. I find a smile playing across my face involuntarily, and I'm only snapped back to reality when I feel a hand on my shoulder suddenly.

I jerk my attention up to see Gerald giving me a knowing smile, and I feel color in my face as I give a quiet scoff and focus on my coffee again. I shouldn't get distracted like this, anyway. We may be out of the frying pan for now, but as the saying goes –

As if on cue, all four of us nearly jump as a loud pounding sound knocks at the door.

CHAPTER 8 - CHERRY

"Oh no," I murmur, scooting over closer to Leon on the floral couch. The police have found us. We've been caught. I glance suspiciously at Gerald and Wanda standing in the kitchen, wondering if maybe they've turned us in. Wanda might have called the cops while we were busy talking to Gerald. I don't want to believe any of that, as the old couple seems so warm and genuine, but in my current state of fear my brain is just searching for someone to blame.

"Who's that there?" Wanda calls out sweetly. She hobbles into the living room, leaning on her cane. When she catches my eye she gives me a wink and a smile. As if she knows exactly what's going on.

The pounding at the door gets louder as a second voice outside shouts, "URGENT BUSINESS ABOUT YOUR FLOWER BEDS!"

At the sound of his voice, I can feel Leon's shoulders relax and his fists unclench. I give him a look of confusion. Why isn't he panicking like I am? What the hell is the cop talking about? Flower beds? Is this some kind of weird, elaborate prank?

Leon stands up and pats Wanda gently on the shoulder as he makes his way to the front door. I want to run after him and pull him away, hide him from the cops. Surely he isn't stupid enough to answer the door himself! Doesn't he know they're here to arrest him? That filthy slimeball Mickey Lamar probably pinned the shooting on Leon and now they're booking him in for attempted murder or something.

"Alright, alright!" Leon says loudly as he turns the front door handle and opens it. I cautiously get up and look around the corner to see Leon facing down a pair of officers.

"What is he doing?" I hiss, biting my lip worriedly. Wanda appears at my side looking very calm and sagacious. She puts a hand on my arm and shakes her head, still smiling.

"Oh, sweetheart, don't worry. It's all under control. They're on our side," she informs me quietly. Gerald comes walking around the corner with his lopsided gait to stand by Leon at the front door.

"What seems to be the matter, fellas?" he asks gruffly. But there's a hint of sarcasm to his voice, like he's simply reading from a script and finding it more than a little amusing.

"Routine business, sir," responds the first officer. "May we step inside?"

"Of course, of course. Anything for the strong and just arm of the law," the old man answers with a deep belly laugh. He stands aside and spreads one arm in a gesture of welcome, and the two officers walk in.

"Let me start a pot of tea and fetch us some sandwiches," Wanda pipes up brightly, taking me by the hand suddenly. "I'm sure you're all famished!" she adds as she nudges me alongside her to the kitchen.

"Thanks, ma'am," says officer number two.

Standing at the little wooden island counter, I lean back to peer around the corner into the living room, where Gerald, Leon, and the two policemen are gathering now, talking in hushed voices. Wanda is humming some upbeat tune as she takes various items out of the cupboards and refrigerator, setting them down on the counter in front of me.

"What the hell is going on?" I whisper urgently. Wanda turns around to face me, beaming. She slides a bagged loaf of bread toward me and sets a butter knife down.

"We're making sandwiches," she quips lightly.

"I can see that," I reply, fighting the urge to roll my eyes. The whole Stepford Grandmother routine is getting old. I just want to know why, after Leon and I took every precaution to avoid being caught, the men are now simply shooting the breeze with a pair of cops in the living room ten feet away.

"Turkey, swiss, lettuce, tomato, and mustard. I suppose that'll do!"

"Why are the cops here?" I ask in an undertone.

"Sorry, dear, I'm a bit hard of hearing!" Wanda shoots back, still preparing the sandwiches as though everything is perfectly normal. This is getting ridiculous.

I drop the loaf of bread and storm into the living room despite Wanda's feeble protests behind me. Walking straight up to circle of men, I demand, "Could someone *please* tell me what's going on right now! Are we under arrest, or what?"

The officers blink confusedly at me, then they both start to chuckle.

"Wow, I've never seen someone so eager to incriminate herself," says the first one, whose name badge reads SAMUELS.

The second one, whose lapel bears the name GREENE laughs, "I wish we were here to arrest you. It'd be an easy job."

"Cut her some slack, gentlemen," Leon interjects, though he's smiling, too. "This is a new friend of mine. She's not fully initiated yet, alright?"

"New friend, eh?" Greene says, waggling his eyebrows up and down and nudging Leon in the ribs.

"You gonna *initiate* her, or ya gonna give us the pleasure?" Samuels jokes. But Leon gives them both warning glares and their smiles fade instantly.

"Drop the innuendoes, boys," Gerald adds, rolling his eyes. "This is serious business, if you haven't forgotten. This is John LaBeau's girl."

Both officers immediately remove their hats and press them to their chests, bowing their heads slightly in deferential courtesy.

"Our apologies, miss."

"And condolences. John was a good man."

"Thank you. He was," I respond, my voice sounding thick and emotional. I have to hold it together. I can't afford to look weak in front of these guys.

"Have a seat, boys!" Wanda says, wobbling into the room carrying a silver tray stacked with turkey sandwiches and little cups of tea. Leon rushes to take it from her gently.

"Here, let me get that," he offers, lifting it away from her with one steady hand. Something moves deep inside me at this kind, simple gesture. Maybe he isn't the cold-blooded gangbanger I thought he was this morning in the warehouse. In fact, that first encounter seems to have happened so long ago, in another world. It's hard to believe that in under twenty-four hours so much has transpired. So much for life moving slow in Bayonne.

"Thank you, son," Wanda says, beaming at him as she settles into a slouchy, ancient-looking armchair.

I wonder how often Leon comes by to see them. I'm sure that the old couple sees something of their own late son in him. My heart aches for their loss. Sure, I have lost my own father, but I can't imagine how terrible it must be to have to bury one's own child. Especially under such suspicious circumstances.

The men all sit down, leaving a spot on the couch beside Leon, presumably for me. So I take it, shivering just so slightly when my thigh touches against his. I force myself not to look down, not to give that minuscule touch even an ounce of my attention. After all, like Gerald said, this is serious business. I'm not here to cuddle up to some hot shot bad boy.

Even if he did literally save me from otherwise certain death so many years ago. And despite the fact that he's scorchingly, blindingly attractive. I can hardly fathom what those muscular arms and sensual lips could do to my body…

Nope! I scream at myself internally. *Focus!*

"So what exactly are you all here for, officers?" Leon asks, resting his elbows on his knees and leaning forward to take a sandwich from the stack.

Samuels, between gigantic bites of his sandwich, replies plainly, "We heard over the dispatcher about the shots fired at Mickey's earlier."

"Had a strong inklin' you were involved," Greene adds.

"Well, you got me. I was there. I might have inadvertently caused it to happen," Leon admits, looking crestfallen and guilty.

"You weren't the one holding the gun," I interject suddenly, before I can stop myself. I can't stand by and let Leon take the fall for what Mickey did.

"Yeah, but I provoked him," he counters with a shrug. "I'm just as guilty as he is."

"Don't martyr yourself for him," I reply, standing my ground.

Greene looks back and forth between us, a little bemused, then he simply asks, "Were there any injuries?"

Leon nods and heaves a burdened sigh. "Yes. One man outside was shot through the window when Mickey's gun went off. He was aiming for me until one of my own men took him down and the gun misfired."

"Is the injured civilian at Bayonne Med?" Samuels asks, changing the topic.

Leon shakes his head. "I'm gonna be honest with you here. The guy who was shot — he's illegal. We didn't wanna risk taking him to a hospital where he might get turned in or something. Besides, he just started working at that asshole's store for less than minimum wage. I don't think he could've handled the costs. Although," he says, brightening up, "I'm fairly certain Mr. Lamar has been convinced to pay for any medical fees the guy will incur. But for now, Anya's got him stashed away somewhere safe, stitching him up."

At the mention of Anya's name, the Lawrences perk up. Wanda clasps her hands together pridefully and says, "Oh, she's such a hero. Our Henry would be so proud of her."

"I knew my son picked a good one," Gerald says, sitting up a little straighter.

"Well, we certainly don't have any intentions of turning him over to Immigration," Samuels says, shaking his head. "But we would like to drop in and check on him after our shift change tonight."

"Just to make sure," Greene says.

"Oh, do tell Anya 'hello' for us, will you?" Wanda pleads.

"Sure thing, Mrs. L," Greene replies with a smile, reaching over to pat her hands.

"So how bad is this, exactly?" Leon asks, sipping his tea with a delicateness that's almost amusing in contrast to his tough-guy looks.

Samuels leans back and sighs. "Well, so far it's nothin' to get too worked up about. Especially if you're sure the injured man is gonna pull through. The FBI's in town, yeah, but they haven't poked their grimy noses too far into our business yet."

"Give 'em some time," says Greene distastefully, rolling his eyes.

"Well, we will just have to make sure we're ready for the *pidarasy* when they do," says Leon, clenching his fist. I can't help but be drawn to the musculature of his arm, the smoldering ferocity in his face. I want to smooth away the tension and see what he looks like totally relaxed, totally vulnerable…

There I go again.

"In the meantime, it's probably still best that you lay low for awhile, Leon," advises Samuels, fixing him with a meaningful stare.

I get the distinct impression that "laying low" is not something Leon does particularly well. He doesn't strike me as the kind of guy who likes working in the shadows, in the background. He's pretty upfront about the things he does, and he clearly doesn't have a lot of concern for his own safety and wellbeing.

"For sure," Greene agrees. "A lowlife like Mickey is gonna blab about this to everyone he meets on the street. Luckily for us, he's such a notorious loudmouth nobody is likely to take him too seriously, anyway."

"You'd think a guy who runs a liquor store in a not-so-upscale part of town would be a little more careful about not pissing off every single person who comes in contact with him, but here we are," laughs Samuels.

"What happened to the gun?" Gerald asks suddenly.

"Taken care of. My right-hand man Genn took it away somewhere out of Mickey's reach. It's been confiscated," Leon concludes, smiling. I know he's remembering Mickey's own accusation of 'confiscating' the weapon earlier today at the liquor store.

"Alright. Well, I guess that just about covers it, then."

Both officers stand up to leave. Samuels says to Wanda, "Thank you for the tea and stuff, ma'am. You're a real treasure to the neighborhood."

"For sure. Always a pleasure to see you," Greene says, nodding.

"Oh, stop it, you!" she giggles, swatting at him playfully.

We walk them over to the front door, and just before the officers disappear down the steps of the brownstone, Samuels points an emphatic finger at Leon and me. "I'm serious about layin' low, alright? Don't show your faces until at least tomorrow. For your own good and ours."

Leon sighs. "Got it, Officer."

Once the cops are gone and we're all standing awkwardly in the living room, Gerald puts his hands on his hips and announces, "Well, looks like you two are staying here tonight."

Leon starts to protest, "Oh, that's not necessary — "

"Yes it is! You two will take the basement room." Wanda insists, getting up from her chair to lay her trembling hands on his arm, a concerned and determined look on her face.

"You heard the missus," Gerald shrugs. "You're our guests for the night. But I promise we will stay out of your hair. Won't we, Wanda?" he adds, giving his wife a meaningful look.

She opens her mouth as though to argue, but then simply sighs instead. "Of course."

"We'll start on supper," Gerald continues, gesturing to his wife. She nods and follows him into the kitchen. Leon gives me an apologetic half-smile.

"Sorry about this," he tells me in an undertone. "You never should've gotten mixed up in this. If you need to sneak out and go somewhere, check in with someone— "

"No," I reply quickly, shaking my head. "There's — there's no one."

Leon blinks a couple times, a little taken aback by my response. I realize too late how pathetic it sounds. That there's nobody waiting up for me. Nobody to worry over when I'm coming home. How depressing.

"Sorry about Gerry and Wanda. They don't get a whole lot of visitors anymore these days, except for when members of the Club stop by. Wanda gets lonely, you know. She's been a little off since Henry passed," he explains softly.

I nod. "That's understandable."

"How are you holding up?" he asks, moving a little closer.

I frown at him for a moment, trying to ascertain what he's talking about. Then it hits me. Obviously he's asking how I'm feeling about my dad's death. I must look cold-hearted. But it's just the way I deal with things. I find ways to distract myself until I'm ready to face the problem head-on, and I'm just not there yet.

"Oh, I'm okay. Yeah, I'm good," I reply, trying to strike a balance between nonchalant enough not to warrant his pity and genuine enough not to look like an emotionless drone.

"Well, if you ever wanna talk about it or —"

"No. Not now. Thank you."

Leon nods slowly, sizing me up. Then he just says, "Well, then, let's go help the Lawrences make dinner. It'll definitely speed up the process."

He shoots me a brilliant, charming grin and we join the old couple in the kitchen to chop up vegetables and beef tips for a pot roast. It's a relief to have something to do with my hands, and I find myself wrapped up in warm, comforting banter. Gerry and Wanda clearly adore each other, and they seem to regard Leon as their adoptive son. Throughout the evening I can't stop smiling. Despite everything that's happened, despite what I've recently lost, I can't help but feel a little bit like I've come home.

*****

"I wonder if they even know how dusty it is down here," Leon jokes as we walk down the stairs into the basement room. It looks exactly like a typical teenage boy's hideaway from the 90s, and I assume sadly that the couple probably haven't even looked down here since Henry's death. It makes sense that they would want to leave it exactly as he left it, even though he was much older than a teenager when he died.

"Looks like a time capsule," I comment, pointing to the curling Nirvana poster on the wall. There's a long-abandoned lava lamp on a rickety little coffee table across the room, the blobs of wax suspended in the same place they were when the lamp stopped working probably decades ago.

"Yeah, when Henry went off to college I think they kinda wanted to keep everything the way he had it, just in case he ever decided to move back in."

"That's sweet."

"Not particularly well-adjusted, but yeah. I suppose it is sweet. They lived for that kid."

"It's hard losing someone who was the center of your world like that," I answer, biting my lip. I can feel Leon staring at me from across the room but I don't want to meet his gaze.

"Oh, hey! Look at this!" he calls out, waving me over excitedly.

"What is it?"

He holds up a big, dust-coated bottle of amber liquid. He rubs the dust off the label and laughs out loud. "It's bourbon. Old as hell. I doubt Gerry even knows it's down here."

"I didn't take him for an aficionado," I reply, bemused.

"He's not. In fact, he was a bit of a boozer when he was a young guy. Wanda told me once that the day they found out she was pregnant with Henry he gave up the bottle for good. That's probably why this stuff is down here. Henry was a good guy, too. Never touched the stuff. I doubt Anya would've let him, anyway," he chuckles.

He opens the bottle and wipes the top off on his shirt. Then he holds it out to me.

"Want the first taste?"

"Oh no. Finder's fee. You first," I reply, grinning in spite of myself.

"With pleasure," Leon says, taking a big swig. He closes his eyes, swallows, and smiles.

He passes me the bottle and we get comfortable on the floor, spreading out the massive mountain of pillows and blankets Wanda supplied for us. We spend the next hour or so just laughing and sharing stories about what it was like growing up in Bayonne, passing the bottle back and forth until it's nearly two-thirds gone.

"Did you ever go to that one bakery off 23rd?" Leon's green eyes are hooded with intoxicated relaxation. He's sitting with his legs straight out, his back propped against a wall of cardboard boxes holding God knows what. I'm across from him with my legs tucked underneath me, my hair falling down around my shoulders.

"Oh, I don't know. Maybe."

"No, no, you'd remember if you did," he laughs. "The woman who ran the counter wore the most obvious platinum blonde wig. She used to draw her eyebrows on with a Sharpie, I swear."

"Give her a break!" I giggle. "It was a different time. I'm sure a lot of people thought she looked damn good."

"Yeah, maybe it's just me," Leon concedes. There's a warm, happy glow to his cheeks.

"So, I have to ask," I start, biting my lip. "Why are you looking into Dad's death?"

"Well, you know, he was starting to come around to us and our way of doing things. He was a stubborn guy, but he had a good heart. Once he realized we're the good guys, he wanted to help. So he did," Leon explains.

"Was he part of the Club?" I ask, trying to remember not to call it a gang. He doesn't seem the sort who'd be okay being associated with that word. But my heart is racing at what he just said. How could I not have known? How could so much have changed while I was off doing my own thing in the big city? Guilt seizes my heart so tightly I feel a physical pang in my chest.

Leon shakes his head. "No, no. Just a sympathizer. He was helping us get information about his employers, as well as gathering intel about similar operations around town."

"And is that… why he died?" I ask quietly.

"That's what I'm trying to find out," he says sadly. "I'm sorry — "

"No," I interrupt, getting up to move closer to him. "I'm sure it wasn't your fault.

You, my dad, the others — I know you were all trying to do the right thing. My dad wouldn't want me blaming the wrong people for his death."

"But if he'd never gotten involved…"

"Then he would have just continued being a cog in the machine like he was his whole life. You obviously gave my dad a new perspective he was passionate about."

"And now you're involved. I don't think… I don't want…" Leon trails off for a moment. Then he finishes, "I don't want to be responsible for getting you in too deep."

"Thanks for the concern, but I'm a big girl," I answer, staring into his green eyes. Suddenly, the electricity that's been growing between us seems to shoot a lightning bolt through my body. I feel hot all over.

"I — I can handle myself," I add. Leon's eyes are focused on my lips and my heart is racing in my chest. Without letting myself second-guess the decision, I dive in and press my mouth against his. Immediately his hands come up to wrap themselves in my hair.

His tongue pushes into my mouth and I moan into his, climbing over to straddle him. His hands fall to grip my hips and hold me there. The taste of bourbon burns in our mouths and my head is fuzzy with pleasant dizziness. I take Leon's face in my hands and kiss him deeply, rolling my hips against the growing bulge in his jeans. I can feel myself getting wet. Even with everything that happened today, I know that in the back of my mind, this moment has been swiftly approaching.

He's the one who reached down and pulled me out of the ocean when I thought I was lost forever. He's the one who rescued me. And now we've found each other again. It has to be fate — some magnetic force of nature that's drawn us back together again so many years later.

We're inevitable.

Leon pushes the hair back out of my face and gathers it over my left shoulder, then leans in to kiss a trail down from my lips, over my neck, to my collarbone. His teeth graze my skin and he sucks delicious, bright-red marks into my flesh, causing me to cry out and push into him longingly. I need to feel his skin on mine. I crave the refuge of his hot, strong body.

He peels his shirt off and tosses it across the room, his lips promptly returning to kiss me again and again. My hands rove up and down his hard, muscular chest and stomach. I can feel every single one of his abdominal muscles defined beneath my wandering fingertips. I can only imagine how powerful he must be, how strong.

The very next moment, I find out.

He picks me up, lifts me easily off of his lap, and lays me down on the blanketed floor on my back before climbing over me and helping me out of my top. He throws it aside and then turns back to sigh hungrily, looking down at my nearly-exposed chest. He slides his fingers underneath the lace of my bra to caress my nipples and grope my breasts. I groan and close my eyes, arching up into his touch. Wordlessly, he lifts me up just enough to reach around and unclasp my bra. Then he tosses that, too.

Leon bends down to kiss me, his hands squeezing and fondling my breasts. I put my arms around him and drag my fingers down his back, clawing needily at him. He responds with a deep, resonant moan. So he likes it a little rough. A little messy.

So do I.

"Vy prekrasny," he murmurs.

"I need you," I whisper back.

He wastes no time taking off his jeans and mine and discarding them into the growing pile of our clothing. I can see the protruding shaft straining in his boxers and I suck in a tight breath at his size. Leon is huge. I can't help but lick my lips in anticipation. I want him inside me, now. I want to feel him filling me up and closing up that void aching within. I need to be distracted, to be embraced wholly. For someone to make me feel wanted and less alone — even if just for one night.

Leon kneels between my legs, hooks a finger under my damp panties, and slips them to one side, leaving my slick flower exposed. He pushes my thighs further apart and dives in between them, his mouth devouring my pussy. His tongue drags up and down my wet slit, flicking now and again over my swollen bud.

"Oh my God," I mumble, clutching at the blankets. What if the couple upstairs overhears us? This is definitely not a position I want Wanda and Gerry to find us in.

But when Leon plunges a finger inside my aching hole I can't suppress a cry of surprise and pleasure. He curls his finger and strokes expertly at that deep, forbidden sweet spot inside of me while his tongue works my clit. It's not long before I'm bucking against his face, my hands making frustrated fists in the blankets on either side of me. I'm moaning and clenching, on the verge of an explosion.

When it comes, Leon doesn't relent, even when I have to clap a hand over my own mouth to stifle a scream as an orgasm shudders through me. It's been ages — probably months — since I last had an orgasm. And even then, I've never had a climax quite like this. My whole body is trembling and weak, but Leon keeps going. He sucks my clit and pushes another finger inside of me, forcing me to keep my legs open even though it almost hurts now.

But pain is the close cousin to pleasure, and a second orgasm comes hurtling toward me, fast. I have to bite my hand to keep from screaming again, and this time Leon withdraws his finger, continuing to gently lap at my juices until I come down. Then he tugs my soaked panties down my legs and throws them before taking off his own underwear. His massive cock springs free, bouncing and erect.

Leon bends down and crouches over me, angling the head of his shaft at my opening and pushing inside with one swift thrust. I arch my back and my head rolls back, my eyes closing. He's enormous and thick and just what I need.

"Ohh, you feel so good," he groans. When I reach up to touch his face, he turns and kisses my palm tenderly, closing his eyes. Then he pins down my arms on either side of me so I can't move them at all. The juxtaposition of such a soft, gentle gesture with this show of dominance is overwhelming, intoxicating. He is both kitten and tiger at once, prince and beast.

He thrusts into me hard, again and again, without mercy. My aching, shuddering cunt envelops him fully, taking him in, right to the hilt. When I feel my third orgasm getting closer, he speeds up the pace, his hips snapping with an arrhythmic frenzy until his mouth falls open and he fixes me with a blazing, green-eyed gaze.

We lock eyes just as he pushes into me and shoots a stream of hot seed deep inside my depths. He groans my name just as I whisper his, my own climax immediately following. He collapses beside me and presses his lips to mine, our arms encircling each other instantly. We press our foreheads together and pant heavily, coming down from the highest of earthly highs.

The two of us fall asleep this way, tangled up together while his hot honey slowly leaks out of me onto the blankets.

CHAPTER 9 - CHERRY

When I wake up to the smell of coffee and bacon wafting from upstairs, it's already ten in the morning. My eyes widen in shock when I see the time on my dying cell phone. I never sleep in this late. Back in New York, I used to always get up early so I could start my commute while some of the city was still asleep. It felt like a normal town with the noise level slightly decreased — well, almost normal. But here in Bayonne, I guess my body just readjusted accordingly with the slower pace of life.

Of course, it's also been a long time since I last had sex.

And last night was definitely enough to wear me out for awhile.

I close my eyes and wince at the thought. I can't believe I slept with him. I've been back in town for less than seventy-two hours and I've already fucked some random guy in the basement of two kindly old strangers' house. What the hell is wrong with me?

Is there a "slutty" phase to the stages of grief?

But then, I remind myself that Leon isn't really a random guy. In fact, there's a stronger connection between the two of us than has ever existed with any of my past boyfriends. We have a history, albeit a vague one. He was the boy who saved me from drowning at the beach when I was a little girl. And he has been investigating my father's death since before I even got here.

Hell, he was probably one of the last people to see my dad alive.

This thought makes that recurring lump in my throat surface again. I sigh and force myself to get up. I rub my eyes and pull my hair back into a messy ponytail to keep it out of my face, then quickly start pulling on my clothes again. I fell asleep naked in the basement of two innocent elderly folks. This is going to be the most ridiculous walk of shame imaginable.

Then it hits me.

My car!

It's still at Mickey's Liquors! How the hell am I going to get back there? What if the police had it impounded? What if Mickey sought revenge and beat the hell out of it or slashed my tires or something? It's a rental, and I definitely can't afford to replace it if anything bad happened. My heart racing, I grab my bag and run up the basement stairs.

"Oh, good morning, dear! Come get some breakfast!" Wanda calls out to me from her perch on the couch. She's watching the morning news, a tray of bacon, toast, and scrambled eggs steaming on the coffee table. She sips from her mug and waves me over.

"I — I'm sorry, I really need to go," I tell her, shaking my head sadly. God, that food smells heavenly. Especially since I have a slight hangover from that bottle of bourbon I split with Leon last night. "I've got to catch a bus or something. My car — "

"It's parked outside," Gerald says, coming around the corner with a newspaper in hand to sit next to his wife.

"Wh-what?" I stammer, furrowing my brow. I know he's getting up there, but surely Gerry's not old enough to be senile yet.

"Yes, yes. That's right. Dear Leon was up before the sun to fetch it along with some of the other darlings from the Club," Wanda says, nodding and beaming.

"Oh," I reply, astonished and relieved. "I never got to tell him thank you."

Gerry looks over at me with his blue eyes twinkling. "I doubt that's the last you'll be seeing of him.You'll get your chance, I'm sure."

I can't help but blush. I hope to God they don't know what went on last night in their basement. Too embarrassed for words, I simply stand there frozen, my mouth hanging open. Wanda swivels around in her spot, waving me over more emphatically.

"I know you've got places to go, but you can't expect to get far on an empty stomach," she scolds me gently. She's adorable in her purple floral nightgown. There are still curlers in her hair and fuzzy slippers on her feet. Gerry has his arm around her, his eyes occasionally flicking over to her warmly. I find the whole scene utterly endearing, and it fills me with a sense of unnameable longing. I want that. I want someone to look at me the way Gerald Lawrence looks at his wife, even after all these decades together. It's like they're newlyweds, the way they dote on each other. I can only hope to find something so precious someday.

I obediently walk over and take a plate, loading it up with food before settling into a chair to watch the morning news with Wanda. There are the usual pieces about lost dogs and weather patterns, new businesses opening and old ones closing. Not a single mention of the liquor store incident. I smile to myself.

Samuels and Greene must have done a hell of a job covering it up.

When I'm finished, I thank the Lawrences profusely, and Wanda holds my hand in both of hers for a solid minute while she tells me how wonderful it was to meet me and how dearly she hopes I will come back to visit again. I assure her, with all honesty, that I certainly intend to.

Then I hoist my bag over my shoulder and head down the front steps to my car parked half a block down. I panic for a moment at the locked door, then realize that Leon must have slipped my keys back into my bag when I hear them jangling. He really thought of everything. My heart skips a beat when I think about the way he held me last night, so tenderly and passionately all at once. I have never been touched that way before.

I wonder if I will ever see him again. I don't have his number or even his full name. All I know is that he's the closest thing to a knight in shining armor I've ever met, and if fate brought us back together once… then just maybe I'll be lucky enough to find him again.

I slide into the driver's seat and pull my bag into my lap to take out a journal I found back at my dad's house. I thrust it into my bag yesterday before I ran out to tail the motorcycle club to the liquor store, and I haven't thought much of it until now. But I take it out of the bag and start poring through the weathered pages, blinking back tears at the sight of my father's familiar handwriting, which is surprisingly neat and legible for a working man. There are pages of mundane observations about the weather, birds that landed in his yard, car troubles he worked out with his mechanic friend, and the frequent mentions of me.

When I turn another page, a folded-up, black-and-white print out of a fashion website I write for falls out into my lap. I pick it up and realize it's an article I wrote about peplum dresses and statement necklaces for autumn. Then I look at the journal page:

I read another fashion blog update written by my daughter. She's so talented, but these editors have her saddled with the most vapid material. I know she can do so much more with her skill and passion. All I really want is for Cherry to be happy. If this is what makes her happy, I will gladly spend the rest of my days printing out her gossip blog articles. I miss her, but I know she's got her own life now in the big city. Things are too dull here for her. She deserves more than Bayonne has to offer, that's for sure.

Finally, after days of holding back, a teardrop falls and stains the paper, blurring my name on the page. I sniffle and hold the journal tight to my chest, closing my eyes and leaning back against the seat. I had no idea my dad was reading all those dumb, silly articles I wrote. I figured he had much better things to do than track down every single useless piece I published. Suddenly I am terribly angry with myself for letting him down. I thought I had years—many years—left to prove my worth to him. I wanted him to live to see me become the writer he knew I could be, the heroic truth-teller he wanted me to be. I never expected to lose him before he got the chance to see me really shine.

And now, no matter how hard I work, he will never know. He died with the knowledge that his only child was nothing more than a puff piece writer. I swipe at my eyes furiously, my chest heaving as I finally let my emotions overwhelm me for the first time since his death. I can't believe I've wasted so much time being anything less than he expected of me. All I want is to be good enough, but instead I've just spent my whole life messing around, taking the road *most* traveled because I'm too afraid to break free of the expectations the rest of the world puts on me. I've been living up to the image of my silly, girly name, instead of fulfilling who and what I really am inside.

Well, that's going to change now.

"I can do better than that, Daddy," I whisper aloud, shaking my head.

I'm going to prove to him that I can be tough, that I can track down the hard, cold truths that people want to keep concealed. I'm going to find out what happened to my father, really. I don't know how I'm going to make it happen, but somehow I am going to make this right.

I look through his journal some more, turning on the radio for some background noise. After pages and pages of the same kind of stuff, I stumble upon a later entry describing something odd. I squint at the page, trying to make sense of the cryptic note:

Commercial field possibly up for sale. Suspect something off. Near the docks. Will coordinate with Volkov to investigate.

"Volkov?" I murmur to myself, trying to figure out if the name is familiar. But it doesn't belong to anyone I can remember from my dad's circle of friends. Maybe it's someone he was working with at the plant. Or maybe… it's someone from the Union Club.

What if it's Leon?

"Calm down," I tell myself, rolling my eyes. I'm clearly just fishing for any reason to think about Leon right now. After all, he did give me the best sex of my life last night. I know there's not much I can do to keep him out of my mind. Those strong arms, his powerful chest, and hard stomach… and that massive, glorious shaft.

I close the journal and toss it in the bag before pressing my face into my palms. I can't afford to be distracted right now! I have way too much to get done. There is a huge mystery surrounding my dad's death and I did *not* come all the way back to Bayonne just to get all googly-eyed for some hot guy. Even if he is really, *really* super hot.

I turn the ignition and start up the rental car, adjusting the seat and mirrors to suit my body. Luckily, whoever drove it over must have been a woman or someone small, since I don't have to adjust anything too dramatically. I wonder if maybe it was Anya.

"Okay. Now where am I going?" I ask myself out loud, biting my lip.

I wrack my brain, trying to figure out what field by the docks my dad could be referencing in his enigmatic note. It's one of the last entries in the whole journal, dated only a week before his death. I don't know if there's any connection, of course, but it's the best lead I have at the moment, so I need to check it out. But where is it?

I've lived outside of town for so long, my memory of the area is a bit rusty. I screw my eyes shut tightly and think hard. *Near the docks.* I used to play around there a lot, riding my bike up and down the sidewalk that runs along the coastline. I hung out with some kids from that part of town who treated the abandoned industrial piping and building materials from deals gone bad like a playground like an obstacle course. We had all kinds of borderline dangerous adventures climbing on top of metal heaps and hiding inside huge cement pipes. That area always needed construction, always looked rundown and forgotten to some extent. And it kind of was.

Then I remember: a field scattered with old auto parts and tires, just a half mile or so from the docks. That has to be it. I used to hang out there as a kid sometimes, picking through the rusting car doors and endless nuts and bolts. My friends and I pretended to be scavengers, like we were going to find all the necessary pieces of a car and build one like Doctor Frankenstein or something. I smile at the memory. What a bunch of dorks.

I think I can still remember how to get there.

Carefully pulling out of the parking spot, I drive off in the general direction of the coast, passing by familiar old buildings and neighborhoods, most of which have fallen into some degree of disrepair. The old general store where I used to buy sodas and pastries looks almost dilapidated now, the roof sinking in from years of harsh weather and not enough funding to get it fixed properly. I shake my head sadly at the state of things. The town I left behind was a quiet one without a lot of prospects, sure, but I never thought I would return to find it in an even bleaker place than I left it.

When I pull up to the field, a wave of memories washes over me. I get out of the car, holding the journal in my hand as I carefully step over the termite-eaten wooden fence. It's barely more than a few stubborn pegs in the grass nowadays, and as I look out over the field, I see that the car parts and tires have been cleared away at last.

"At least somebody tried to help out a little, I guess," I mumble to myself.

But what could be the "something off" my dad suspected? His journal entry is short, but it's easy to see that he was concerned about something going on here. I wonder if he ever made it out here to check. And if he did, what did he find?

Then I see it. Up ahead, there's a wide patch of overgrowth that looks… strange. Unnatural. The whole field is overgrown, of course, but that particular part doesn't look the same. I approach it quickly, tucking the journal under my arm. Up close, I can see that someone has obviously dragged a bunch of ripped-up plants and underbrush from somewhere else and dumped it here. I kick my way through this shoddy covering to see a plot of recently upturned earth. The dirt looks rather freshly placed, as though someone were trying to bury something.

"What the hell?" I breathe, my heart starting to pound.

Did I just find a shallow grave?

I start to feel dizzy and sick to my stomach so I immediately turn and bolt back to my car. I don't know what could be buried there, but I know one thing for sure: I am going to find out.

CHAPTER 10 - LEON

I can't get her out of my head. The more I try to push the thought away, to stuff the feelings into the same box I shoved all the rest of my good memories of this town before it all went to hell, it just floats right back up to the surface, harder and stronger than before.

She's something else entirely. For her to come back into my life here, now, with everything that's going on, I feel like I'm trying to ride out a storm inside me. I've always been the one who can handle these kinds of things. This is unbelievable. I'm the president of the

Union Club, and one woman from my adolescence gets me turned inside out. She's getting in my way in more ways than one, and the only thing worse than that is the fact that I don't think I mind her doing so very much at all.

Right now, I'm trying to get the thought of her out of my mind while I read over research on James & Son Realtors, a company that's trying to sell off that big plot of land near the water. Keeping tabs on local realty isn't something an MC leader is known to get involved in, but then again, not many MCs look out for local affairs as closely as the Union Club does.

This particular plot of land is a big sell. It's in a prime location for commercial activity, it's close to the water, and it's big enough to be split into a handful of local businesses, but the city has kept it as one big parcel and just sat on it for a long time.

Part of that is our doing. Lots like this tend to be ready-made for big national business to draw in revenue. Lot gets sold off to some mega-corp from out of town, a huge store gets erected on the spot, and before you know it, most of the jobs in town get filtered into that one location, lining corporate pockets and driving local business owners to their doorstep. We've taken it upon ourselves to make sure, one way or another, that realty agents like James & Son don't sell them off. Worker collectives can do wonders for political change on a local level. *The things you figure out as an MC leader*. We'd been about to start pushing for the city to split up the lot into smaller parcels to sell off to local upstart businesses, before the FBI decided to show up.

My best guess is that their presence is what's emboldened the realty agency to sell.

Fuck, this is frustrating work. I'm not made to sit at a desk all day when I could be out on the streets getting shit done.

I try to bat those thoughts away, but they keep getting in the way like flies.

Cherry would be great at this kind of investigative stuff.

I take a drink of my beer as I try to dispel that thought. Not many people get in the way of me and my club anymore, but it wasn't always like that. When we were first starting out, the skeezy business owners would discretely try to hire thugs to threaten us, find dirt to blackmail us with, even come start fights at The Glass. I've had to fight a man off in front of the very desk I'm sitting at in the bar's office in the back. The desk still has a chip in it where the man's knife hit.

The fact of the matter is that this is dangerous work we're doing, especially with the FBI breathing down our necks now. I don't want Cherry to get wrapped up in all that.

I rub my temple. *Who am I kidding? I'm not getting anything done tonight*. Why do I even care so much about Cherry, though? She's basically an out-of-town stranger at this point, right? Yet she's slipped right into the swing of things as if she'd never left. She's a liability, isn't she?

Well, actually, even acting alone with no resources, she's been keeping up with our entire club every step of the way. She's a natural. Even the way she handles herself on a motorcycle feels like she was meant to be there. She's got every bit of the fire I do to dive right into things at the first whiff of foul play. She's got even more of a stake in the murder investigation, and she's handled herself like a professional more than once.

I feel a pang in my chest as I realize how much I've been thinking about her. *What's gotten into you, Leon?*

I've got to shake myself out of it. But fuck, it's been a hell of a ride on my own, trying to fight upstream against what seems like the whole institution lined up against me. The patch members and my officers, they're truer brothers and sisters to me than any flesh-and-blood siblings ever could be. I couldn't ask for a tighter group to ride with, and we'd all take a bullet for each other if it came to that.

To meet someone else, a ghost from brighter days, storming into town with all the tenacity and fire I had when I was just starting out, looking like a vixen with eyes and lips that could knock a man out, and a body so stunning I can still feel it when I think about her...

"Hey, boss?" I hear Eva's voice from behind the door with a light knock before she lets herself in. "Still tied up in all that paperwork?"

Snapping out of my thoughts, I grunt in response, setting my beer aside and leaning back. "Kill me. We ought to hire a suit to take care of this kind of work for us."

"Might not need to," she says with a smile. "we just got a tip from one of the maintenance workers at James & Son."

"You're shitting me," I say, sitting up with a sudden smile. I can't express how done I am with dealing with this paperwork, and I'm eager to get out on the streets again.

"Apparently he overheard a meeting with the bosses. It's a definite lead, but you're not gonna like it. They're trying to sell to NexaCo."

I feel fire burning in my chest, and my hand clenches. They aren't fucking around. NexaCo is the big leagues.

It's a superstore corporation that has branches all over the United States. There's even been talk of them spilling into Canada, but there's been a ton of pushback up there. Having a NexaCo in town spells death for any local businesses that don't have hefty backing from somewhere else. They drive consumer prices into the ground, making competition basically impossible, to the point that NexaCo gets to dictate the prices they pay to their suppliers and shipping companies. They're single handedly responsible for the fall in farmers' wages over the past few years, and I don't want to think about what they'll do to the workers at the docks here in Bayonne.

Worse yet, the company employs one of the most highly trained divisions of union busters in the country. So much as a whisper of collective action, and corporate descends on a branch like the hammer of the gods.

Not in my town.

"That's all I need," I say, standing up and striding around the desk. Eva follows me out the door as I step out into the bar, where a couple of the members give me respectful nods, happy to see me emerge from that lair.

"Alright, everyone," I shout, "listen up! James & Son are bringing NexaCo to town if we don't do anything about it. So we're gonna go have a chat with them."

There's an angry shout of agreement from everyone in the bar, beers and pool sticks raised high.

"Eva, Genn, you're with me. We're gonna go have a talk with them 'quietly.' The rest of you, go make some noise close to Mickey's. It's far enough away that if the feds catch a whiff of you, they won't be paying attention to where the real business is. Just don't answer any questions if you get pulled over, and remember which of the boys in blue are on our take, got it?"

"You got it, Prez," shouts one of the members. A few moments later, half the club is gearing up to get moving, and I take a deep breath.

This is what I live for.

*****

We're riding again, this time for what feels like a more white-collar meeting than our trip to the liquor store. Well, not for us—we normally don't go storming into realty offices like this.

Our bikes pull up at an office building with a nice exterior garden plan. It's got a fountain outside and everything.

"James & Son Realtors," Eva says as she pulls up beside me in the parking lot, Genn pulling up a couple of seconds later. "Nice place. Wonder if they're busy this time of day?"

"Nah," I say back, "most of them will be out to lunch right about now."

"Good," Genn says, cracking his knuckles, "I'd like a little one-on-one time with someone right about now."

"Only a couple of cars in the parking lot," I point out. "Whoever brought lunch from home today is going to get a rude interruption, hate to say. Let's go."

We push the door open and let ourselves inside, making a quick and direct path to the nearest open office door we can spot.

"E-excuse me?" the secretary at the front desk tries to say as we stride past.

"We're expected," Genn says with a friendly smile as we walk by, and the secretary just gapes for a moment before giving up. The balding, white-collar scrub inside the office we make our way to looks up from the sandwich he's eating, and his face goes pale at the sight of us.

"C-can I help you three?"

"Yes, we'd like to arrange a meeting, immediately, if you've got an opening," I say, standing in the middle of the room with my arms crossed as Eva and Genn flank me.

"Y-yeah, I guess I can squeeze you in," he stammers, sweating at the forehead before taking a deep breath and getting his bearings. "You're from the Union Club, aren't you?"

My face splits into a grin. It feels good to get a little recognition every now and then. "And you must be one of the lackeys opening the doors for NexaCo to stroll up in here, huh?"

"Now sir," the man says, holding a hand out as if trying to explain, but there is a definite edge of condescension to his voice, as though he's explaining down to someone. "NexaCo has a complicated reputation, but besides the fact that we're just agents carrying out a sale that's been trying to go through for *years*, the jobs that NexaCo could bring into this city are—"

"Underpaid, without benefits, and designed to drive the local competition to the poor house," I finish for him. "Unlike yours, I'd be willing to bet, but you don't have to think about that on a day to day basis, do you?" I add with a wink.

His face is still, but he looks nervous.

I continue, "Now I know the town's newest guests from Washington make you think we'd change our tune, but just to be clear that isn't the case, I thought we'd drop by to—"

I'm cut off as the man leaps from his office chair, making a mad dash for the door to bolt out the office. Genn catches him at the waist as he tries to slip by, and as he loses his footing, he smacks his head against the side of the doorframe and starts kicking his legs, knocking over some of the office equipment on the desk, I catch a snippet of the voices up front.

"I'm sorry, the only person in the office i-is tied up w-with something right—"

"Okay, yeah, I know them, now just let me get past so I can—"

I know that voice. "Cherry!" I shout out from the office, and it goes quiet up front a moment, the only noise being Genn's grunting with the agent in his grasp. "Hey, you two got a handle on this guy?"

Genn gives a stoic nod, and I return it before slipping around them and making my way out the door and down the hallway to see a flustered-looking Cherry standing beside the distraught secretary.

"Leon, what the hell's going on here?" Cherry has to keep her volume in check, despite the shouting from the office behind us.

"Look, I know what this looks like. We— one sec. Miss?" I turn to the secretary, slipping a $50 out of my pocket and setting it on the front desk. "Give us some privacy and go get lunch, will you? You can tell 'em we threw you out."

The secretary looks hesitant for a moment, then takes the money and gives a curt nod before shuffling out.

"As I was saying," I try to continue with a coy smile, but Cherry doesn't look amused.

"Save it, Leon," Cherry almost snaps, "this is too far."

"Is it?" I say, genuinely surprised. "The weasels who work here are capable of doing a lot more harm than skeezes like Mickey, you know."

"That's not what I mean, and you know it," Cherry says, pacing around the room. "I know why you're here, Leon, and this is insane. You claim you're trying to protect the people in this city, but by all means, tell me how busting up a land sale to keep a shallow grave hidden constitutes 'helping' anyone but yourselves?"

The words hit me out of nowhere, and I just stare at her, dumbstruck for a few moments. "...huh? The hell are you talking about?"

"I went to the plot of land these people are trying to sell, Leon," she says, taking out her phone and showing me the county appraiser's website. "I found out who's selling it, as well as the fact that it's been on the market for ages. And I just stopped by there. I saw the grave, Leon."

"Wait wait wait," I stop her, shaking my head, trying to wrap my mind around what I'd just heard. "What's this about a grave? Cherry, what'd you see?"

Cherry looks long and hard into my eyes, and for a moment, I almost forget she's accusing me of murder. It's an intense gaze that holds me still for a moment, and as I look back into hers, I wonder if she feels the same as I do.

"You really don't know, do you?" she says, her shoulders lowering just a bit. "Oh my God, you don't. Leon, you need to come out there with me. I think this is more serious than we know."

Now it's my turn to rub my hand over my face, thinking quickly. "That doesn't make any sense, though. If they're trying to sell the land off, if there's really somebody buried there, they'll find them the minute they start setting up for construction. Unless…"

Cherry watches my face for a few moment, then the light of understanding sparks in her eyes, and she blanches. "Unless someone *knows* there's a grave there."

My eyes meet hers, and I give her a hard look before nodding curtly. "The FBI may be in town to do more than intimidate us. Come on, follow us back to the bar. I'll get the two in the back to finish up and follow us. As soon as it's night, we're paying the lot a visit.

*****

The grave we find that night is plain as day. I stand over it with my arms crossed while a few patches from the club patrol around us. Cherry is pointing a few things out on the site.

"I've moved a few things around—it wasn't as plainly outlined as it is here, but this is clearly disturbed dirt, about six by two, and there was brush covering it when I found it."

The moonlight is scarce, but it casts just enough light for us to see.

"Only one way to know for sure," I say, and Genn steps forward from behind me with a shovel in hand. Cherry looks horrified.

"Are you kidding? What do you think you're doing? We can't just…"

"I know, but would you rather involve the cops?" I ask, a grim look on my face. Cherry looks reluctant, but finally, she steps back and lets Genn get to work.

He's a tough bull of a man, so it doesn't take long before his careful digging uncovers something, and he sets the shovel aside to start parting the dirt with his hands. As he starts to uncover the body, my brow furrows, and Cherry covers her mouth with a hand.

"Oh my God…"

I was expecting whatever we exhumed to be a body I recognized—someone the mob had dealt with a while ago, or maybe some unsolved murder case locally. But no.

The face in the shallow grave was foreign; clearly someone from south of the border.

"I've heard of this kind of thing happening in Texas," Cherry breathes, "but all the way up here?"

"Prez!" calls one of the men from a dozen feet or so away. "Got another one over here!"

"Here too!"

Now it's my turn to go pale as I sweep across the field with the men to see the extent of what we're standing on. There are over a dozen men and women buried here, all immigrants.

"What do we do, Prez?" Genn asks, kneeling over the grave after looking down on the poor man with a sorrowful look. "We can't go to the cops with this, can we?"

"On the contrary, Genn," I say, a stony expression on my face, "that's exactly what we're going to do."

"What?" Cherry asks, shocked. "After all that talk about keeping the police out of this? Land disputes are one thing, but Leon...this is serious. Really serious. A full-blown investigation could get out of hand. If you were worried about the FBI being in town, this would have them swarming all over us."

"I don't think they came to town to investigate this, though," I say, crossing my arms and looking the dead man in the face. "So we're going to play them at their own game. We'll make this public, and we'll kill two birds with one stone—we'll get justice for the victims here with unmarked graves, and making this place a crime scene will shut down the NexaCo branch for so long they won't even want it by the time they're finished investigating."

Cherry seems uncertain for a while, but finally, her expression softens, and she nods. "It's risky...but these people need justice. I'll bet there are some families that want closure over this, too."

A smile tugs at my face as I look at her. "I agree. Alright everyone," I say to the patches around me, "let's clean up and head back. Come tomorrow, we're doing something the Union Club has never done before. We're gonna reach out to the police."

CHAPTER 11 - CHERRY

Going to the police this morning was nerve-wracking. I have been fortunate — or boring — enough to never have a real run-in with the cops. Even in the crime-laden city of New York, I managed to stay on the straight and narrow, keeping my business to myself. I've never had so much as a noise complaint or a parking ticket in all my years on this earth, and it's a point of pride for me. So walking into the police station in Bayonne was terrifying. A totally unfamiliar experience.

Especially since I was there to report a murder.

Granted, the detective I spoke to was quick to assure me that the case could not definitively be labeled a homicide until a full investigation and autopsy were completed. Which is police slang for: "Okay, crazy lady, you're the fifth person today to walk in here all wide-eyed trying to report some bizarro crime just for the attention." The detective, who introduced herself as Maria Hanson, took down my name and details on a little chart.

"Name?" she prompted, not looking up from the clipboard.

"Uh, Cherry LaBeau."

She immediately looked up, a flicker crossing her dark features. I waited for the usual incredulous *"Cherry? Really? Your name is actually Cherry?"* But it never came. And then I realized she was noticing my *last* name. Because my father recently died. I didn't get a chance to ask about his case — or whether the police even had a case for him — before she reassumed her previous nonchalance and continued the interview.

Detective Hanson took all my information and nodded through my description of the shallow grave on the NexaCo plot of land. She did raise an eyebrow at my explanation of the upturned earth and shoddy attempts to cover it up. Of course, I don't tell her that Union Club members exhumed the body themselves just to make sure. I conveniently left that part out. I had a strong inkling that the cops wouldn't be too pleased with the prospect of civilians digging up bodies in the middle of the night. Especially civilians who happen to have a rough relationship with the authorities. I hoped she would believe me, at least enough to get a team out there to check it out.

And luckily, she did.

Now I'm standing in the field with my hands on my hips, biting my lip nervously as the forensics team starts the exhumation process. There's a group of several guys with digging equipment, along with a couple of skeptical cops standing around shooting the breeze. I can tell they all think this is most likely a waste of time.

"You sure there's a human body down there?" pipes up one of the cops, a fresh-faced young rookie with a name badge that says WILLIS. The older, paunchy man next to him elbows Willis in the ribs.

"Could just be some poor kid's dead dog or something," he adds gruffly. His badge says his name is NELSON. I want to slap both of them for joking around about this.

Detective Hanson is here, as well, instructing the forensics team and taking down information. She's a tall, soft-spoken black woman with a graceful presence. I hope to God she's one of the good ones, because she seems to actually have some idea of how serious this is.

"Alright, let's get started," she calls out, holding her clipboard under her arm. She gives me a respectful nod and goes off to chat with the two cops, likely to chastise them for being so flippant about a homicide accusation.

The team starts digging, and I bite my nails anxiously, waiting for the first body to turn up. Sure enough, before long that first body we found is uncovered. "Got one, Detective!" shouts the digger. I glance over just in time to see Willis's face go white as a sheet before he faints. Nelson catches him in his arms before the rookie falls completely to the ground, and in any other situation the sight would have been rather funny — a dignified old cop romantically cradling the swooning body of a younger officer.

But in context of the number of dead bodies turning up in this field… I can't exactly blame the guy for passing out, especially since he's clearly new to the job. He can't be more than nineteen years old. I'm sure they've only got him out here as a kind of hazing process, to see if he can handle the dark side of being a cop. From the looks of it, the answer is a resounding no.

"Wake up, kiddo," Nelson says to Willis, patting the kid's cheek and jostling his blue-suited body to jolt him back to reality. The younger cop wakes up slowly, looks around to see at least a dozen bodies have already been exhumed, and he immediately claps a hand to his mouth and runs off to vomit.

Poor kid. Nelson sighs heavily, shaking his head with embarrassment.

"Ah, yeah. Everyone reacts uniquely to their first stiff," comments one of the forensics guys flippantly, shrugging.

"I never fainted at the sight of a corpse!" Nelson retorts, puffing out his chest indignantly.

"I did, my first time," Detective Hanson says. "But to be fair, it was covered in blood. Really nasty scene. But these guys here are pretty clean except for, you know, the dirt and everything. He'll be okay, though. Just give him a minute to pull his shit together."

"I hate rookies," Nelson mumbles, walking away to check on his unfortunate partner.

Beyond the din of digging equipment and shouting voices, I hear a distant rumble approaching. The unmistakable grumble of the motorcycle club getting closer. I hoped they would stay away from the scene, keep their noses clean for the time being. I certainly don't want them to be dragged into this any more than necessary, and I worry that the cops will not take me as seriously if they know I'm working with the Club. But of course they can't stay out of it. I should have expected this.

"Look who's here!" yells Nelson from the corner of the field where he's patting Willis on the back comfortingly. He points to the road, where the motorcycles are pulling off into the grass. A bunch of the members are here, including Leon. My heart does a little skip at the sight of him — both in concern and something like giddiness.

Calm down, Cherry. You're literally surrounded by corpses. Try not to seem too eager to climb all over this hot guy right now.

I grit my teeth and cross my arms over my chest, trying not to look overly interested in their arrival. Detective Hanson swears under her breath and starts jogging toward them.

"You can't come in here, people! This is a crime scene! No onlookers, please."

"We're here to help out," Leon tells her, holding his hands up innocently.

"Like you 'helped out' Mickey Lamar the other day? I don't think so. Come on, don't make me call for backup, guys. Just turn around and leave," Detective Hanson warns them.

"So there's going to be an investigation, right?" Leon counters, changing the subject.

"Yes, yes. But you know I can't give details. So just head on outta here and watch the evening news tonight, okay? I'm sure those media vultures will have stuck their noses all up in this case by then, anyway," she replies, exasperated. "Speaking of which, please keep this information to yourselves, alright? The last thing we need is community panic clouding our investigation and taking up our already limited resources."

"We really just want to help," Genn adds earnestly.

"I swear," Leon tells her, standing his ground. "*Obeshchayu*."

"Thank you for your concern," the detective begins slowly, "but we've got it covered."

Just then, a big black sedan with dark windows pulls over into the grass and a tall, thin man in a suit and thin spectacles gets out. He straightens his jacket and tie and starts walking toward the scene of the crime, his face pinched and serious.

I look over to see Leon's own expression go sour and his hands curl into fists at his sides as he watches the suit approaching. "Really? The feds got a whiff of blood and decided to send their best hound dog out to fetch a case?" he calls out bitterly.

The suited man gives him a flat, unconcerned look, even though it's apparent to me that the two are acquainted in one way or another. I wonder to myself if this is another detective or possibly someone higher up.

Detective Hanson also looks defensive and angry. She puts her hands on her hips and purses her lips, her eyes narrowing with displeasure. "This is our jurisdiction, Agent Doyle. As I was just telling these concerned citizens here, the Bayonne precinct has this case covered. It's ours, Agent. You can tell the FBI we don't need a babysitter."

"I'm sure you're perfectly competent, Detective," answers the suit, "but this case is under our thumb now. The Federal Bureau of

Investigation fully appreciates your participation and hard work regarding this matter up until now, but we will be handling the case from here on out."

"And what if we refuse to stand down?" Hanson rebuts, taking a step closer. I'm amazed at her ability to stay tough and collected in the face of an FBI agent. I, however, am quietly shrinking away. I'm not a fan of cops, and I am definitely in no position to tangle with the FBI.

"Then you will be forcibly removed from the case by whatever means necessary, with a reprimand to your commanding officer," the agent answers coolly.

"Our forensics team is the one out there getting their hands dirty digging up bodies, not yours," Hanson shoots back defiantly. "We're the ones using our resources and time to get this done while you just conveniently show up just as all the bodies are accounted for. You don't like to work very hard, do you, Agent? No, you much prefer to ride up on your high horse just in time to steal all the credit and tell us little guys to go home."

"You're crossing a line, Detective."

"And you're trampling on one!" she hisses.

"I've seen your record, Hanson. Pretty clean so far. It would be a real shame to mar such an excellent record with an insubordination mark."

Detective Hanson bristles at this, glaring at the agent with hatred burning in her dark eyes. Then she finally looks away, shaking her head angrily. "Fine. You want it? Get your own team out here. And good luck tracking down suspects without the assistance of the local PD. We know this town like the back of our hands — its secrets, its idiosyncrasies. The people know us. They'll never open up to an outsider in a luxury car like you," she says.

I look over to see a fleet of more black sedans squealing to a stop on the side of the road, more agents in sunglasses and black suits approaching quickly, looking like serious business.

"Well, as our main suspects have been so considerate as to go ahead and show up to the scene of the crime, I doubt we'll have much trouble taking them into custody," the agent replies, gesturing toward the Club. My stomach drops. They're going to arrest Leon! As if he really has anything to do with this gruesome scene!

"No!" I shout before I can stop myself, running over to Leon. He shakes his head at me, his beautiful green eyes wide and emphatic, telling me to stay out of it.

"Who is this?" the agent asks.

"Our informant," Hanson answers him reluctantly. "She's not involved."

"Well, if she hinders our investigation in any way she will most certainly be considered 'involved' and I will not hesitate to arrest her for obstruction," he says darkly.

I hate the way he talks about me as though I'm not here. I want to turn and tell the Union Club to run, to escape however possible. But they are all standing here quietly, allowing themselves to be arrested! Leon's jaw is clenching and I know it's hurting every fiber of his being to acquiesce so easily to the police.

I wonder why they're not fighting it.

The men in suits start cuffing the Club members, reading them their Miranda rights and leading them away to the cars. When one of them comes up to Leon with a pair of handcuffs out, something snaps in me and I wrap my arms around Leon's body tightly.

"Don't take him, please! He's innocent! They all are, I swear!" I cry.

"I thought you said she was not involved," the agent says impatiently.

"Miss LaBeau, please step back!" Detective Hanson orders.

"I won't let you arrest him when he's done nothing wrong!" I retort, shaking my head. Leon gives me a panicked look.

"No, Cherry. Let me go. Don't give them any reason to drag you in, too," he murmurs to me gently. "I'll be alright. It's just for questioning, they have nothing on me. *Ne volnuytes, kroshka*. It will be okay."

Reluctantly, I release him just as the suited guy pulls Leon's arms behind his back to cuff him and start pulling him away. I run after them a few steps and the first agent follows after me. Leon shouts, "Leave her out of this! She's not involved!"

"Leon!" I yell, panicking. I hate seeing him hauled off in cuffs like this. He's a good guy! I want to turn and scream at the detective, tell her that we're on the right side, beg her not to let the FBI take this over and cover the whole thing up.

The agent grabs my arm and I gasp at the tight grip. Leon goes ballistic, suddenly kicking and struggling to break away from the guy holding him. "Get your grimy paws off her, you piece of scum!" he shouts. "Leave her alone. Don't touch her, Doyle!"

Agent Doyle lets me go hesitantly, leaning in to hiss at me, "Keep out of this. The FBI thanks you for your cooperation and input, but you're no longer needed. Please leave before I'm forced to bring you in for questioning, as well."

"They're innocent! You're arresting the wrong people!" I reply, my voice wavering.

"That is for the Bureau to decide, not you. Now get out of here or I will be forced to arrest you, too. Do not make me ask you again."

We stare at each other for a long, tense moment.

Then some voice in the back of my head reminds me that I won't be much help to the Club, to Leon, if I get locked up myself. So as much as it pains me, I walk away, storming off to my rental car with my heart pounding nearly out of my chest. I get into my car just as the black sedans are pulling away with the Club members in tow.

Starting my engine, I decide to follow them straight back to the precinct. I am **not** going to let them get away with this.

CHAPTER 12 - LEON

Agent Doyle paces back and forth in the interrogation room in the shadows cast by the fluorescent light that's hanging over me as I sit handcuffed at the table. His steps are slow. Painfully slow.

The agent and I go way back. He's been keeping tabs on the Union Club since we first got started. I've had my suspicions that he had a hand in busting the union up in the first place, or at least that he saw some of the money that got spread around after the bust. Maybe it was planned from the start, or maybe some cash was pushed his way to make sure the bosses had the government's support in the fallout, but whatever the case may be, Agent Charles Doyle seems to take special pleasure in putting the twist on all of us.

"You can keep quiet as long as you like, Mr. Volkov, that's well within your rights, but that's only going to make it look worse for you when I present our evidence in court, you know."

I just stare him down, my face unmoving. I know he's just trying to goad me into saying something stupid and incriminating. He's got a file on me six inches thick back up in Washington, and he knows how to press my buttons.

More importantly, I know for a fact he's got nothing on me. We didn't leave a trace of our presence at the scene—Eva made sure of that. And there's not a scrap of DNA they'll be able to pick up on at the scene.

"Now, I don't know what you're doing to 'inspire' those supposedly loyal lackeys of yours running around on overpriced scooters, but that big bearded guy you call your Sergeant at Arms? We've already placed him at the scene, and when we showed him what we've got on him, he started spilling his guts for a deal. We can offer you the same, you know."

A lie. Even as Doyle takes a seat on the table with one leg, peering at me with those still, eerie eyes of his, I can see the lie in them as plain as day. But Doyle isn't the kind of guy to lie out of his ass, so I humor him a little.

"He's not much of a talker on a good day."

"No, but he didn't need to. The mud caked on his bike pedals did most of the talking for him."

I keep a stony face, pretending to be disconcerted, but it's at best a circumstantial piece of evidence. Bayonne's a muddy place.

"Big guy like Gennedy comes in handy moving people around quickly, I'd bet," Doyle says, flipping through a few files in his hands with a smile. "Did he come in handy when you paid Mr. Mickey Lamar a visit and shot one of his immigrant workers, too?"

Doyle very badly wants me to defend myself by pointing out that it was Mickey's gun that was fired; that would make it easy as cake to implicate me as having knowledge that one of the immigrants was going to get shot that day. But I'm not going to let him have that satisfaction.

Doyle looks at me for a long time, as if trying to pry into my mind and take the words from my mouth.

"Stare at me as long as you want, Chuckie, but I don't think all that time behind a cushy desk in Washington is doing much for your psychic powers. Or are you trying to have an intimate moment with me?" I grin, but Doyle's face is immobile. He just stares for another moment before standing up and walking away from me, flipping through those folders again.

"Mr. Enrique Medina was his name. He's on his way to a full recovery, since your first aid made sure it didn't end with a witness to a murder—very nice thinking, by the way. But I wonder, when you went to go terrorize Mickey Lamar at his place of business, before Miss Cherry LaBeau happened to stumble in on the scene as an accomplice, did you mean to kill off the immigrant workers to free up the job for locals—white locals, I should add—or were you not willing to kill two birds with one stone just yet?"

There's not a chance in hell I'm going to say a word in response to that loaded question. Doyle's a shrewd man with an arsenal of verbal traps. There's no winning when answering his questions. I made sure the whole crew was drilled on that the moment I heard he was in town.

"Did I hit a nerve, Mr. Volkov? Or is that just something in your eye?"

I hadn't even realized it, but my fists had clenched at the mention of Cherry's name. I quietly pray he doesn't notice that the thought of her getting dragged into this is what set me off.

"In any case, if you're insisting on being so reticent, I won't mind bringing the ACLU into the investigation as well? They like to keep abreast of reports of white supremacist biker gangs, you know."

It takes every ounce of strength in me not to respond to that by kicking the table into that pencil-necked paper pusher as hard as I can.

"The ACLU and our **club** has a history of cooperation," I say in a guarded tone, "and we've supported justice in Bayonne for years."

"Really?" Doyle retorts without missing a beat, "because the seventeen dead Mexicans in the ground and the one in the hospital seem to tell a different story."

I don't breathe a word of the fact that the worker at the liquor store knows why we really came to the store that day. If they knew that poor worker could testify in our favor, there'd be no way he'd survive his treatment. But the threat of white supremacist accusations could be lethal to all of us, and Doyle knows it. It's a low blow. Not only would it turn the black and Mexican clubs from neighboring areas against us, but the publicity Doyle would see to would turn the public against us. I'm not giving him any ammunition for that, so I hold my tongue.

After a few long, drawn-out moments, Doyle clicks his tongue and sighs. "You're digging your own grave with your silence, Mr. Volkov. And as long as she's supporting you in all this, Miss LaBeau is digging her career's grave, too."

I can't help but clench my jaw, and I glare daggers at Doyle. He seems bemused. He's lucky I'm restrained.

"What, you didn't think I'd look into her, too? Upstart journalist living in the city, Bayonne native, comes down to help out some old friends cover their tracks during what's quickly becoming a large-scale murder investigation? That doesn't sound suspicious in the least to you? I'm sure it will to a jury, that's for sure."

"She's an outsider. She isn't involved with any of this."

"Oh? And could you clarify what 'this' is, precisely? It's looking more and more like a hate crime by the minute."

I've said too much already, and Doyle's snide smile tells me he knows it. He's gotten under my skin, but he still doesn't have anything hard. He's just trying to bait me. That's what I have to tell myself to keep the fire in my heart in check.

"In any case, being a suspected accomplice to a bunch of white supremacists is a nail in the coffin of any journalist trying to make it in New York City, of all places," he says with an insufferable laugh. "But you know, if she goes down, it's just another tragic casualty to keep your **gang** of, ah, motorcycle enthusiasts. All for the crew, right? I mean, like you said, she's an outsider." He grins, and I just narrow my eyes at him. "But it's not as though that's the only thing that woman could run into to put her career in the grave in a town like this.

"Those lines are starting to sound a lot like threats, Charlifer."

"Goaded so easily, Mr. Volkov? I'm sorry, I didn't realize she was that close to you."

"Let's quit beating around the bush, Doyle, you and I know each other a little too well to act like this is a first date. I got word that you were in town a few days before anyone reported anything about either the victims at that plot of land or whatever disturbances Mr. Lamar says went down at the liquor store. What's a Washington hotshot like you doing in our little dried-up dock town? Can't imagine you were here investigating reports that hadn't happened yet. Unless I was wrong about that 'psychic' thing." I raise my eyebrows and tilt my head in as though that's a very real possibility.

"Keeping tabs on me, are you?" Doyle retorts with a smile, sitting down in the chair across from me and folding his hands on the table. "Now *that's* very interesting. I'll answer that if you tell me if you were watching out for law enforcement before or after you started burying dead immigrants in an unoccupied lot?"

He's gotten sharper since the last time we met.

"Funny thing is," I go on, leaning back, "some of the bosses around town got *real* bold when word spread that you were around.

In fact, word spread pretty quick. I always thought the FBI liked to keep quiet when they were stretching out the long arm of the law."

Doyle chews on his cheek, giving me a thoughtful look. "When someone announces themselves, Mr. Volkov, I'd guess it's usually to send a message. I think that much is clear, don't you?"

"Crystal," I say, unfazed. "But after all these years, Chungles, I guess I'm just bitter I still don't know why, when you've got your nice and fancy office in Washington and tons of bigger fish than us to fry, you're still so goddamn insistent on trying to strangle our little slice of New Jersey 'till you feel its last breath of life fogging up those new glasses of yours?"

The agent's eyes are unreadable for a moment. "I'm not here to ruin your little vanity project of a town, Mr. Volkov," he says in a low tone. "If you weren't busy riding bikes around all day, you might notice that it's already ruined." He leans in with an expression as placid as the docks at night.

"I'm just here to put a bullet in its head so the rest of us can move on with our business."

CHAPTER 13 - CHERRY

I have spent more time in this police station over the past couple of days than I ever expected to, collectively, for one whole lifetime. After the big scene at the grave site, I tailed the black sedans to the precinct and watched helplessly from the parking lot as the FBI suits dragged Leon and the rest of the Club into the building. I decided then and there to wait this out. I was determined to stick around until they were inevitably released again.

Of course, that was over twenty-four hours ago now.

I'm still sitting in the waiting room of the police building, waiting for Leon to come out of the interrogation room where they've been holding him for so long. I'm pretty sure, from the true crime shows I've watched, that they can't keep him more than twenty-four hours just for questioning. If they want to hold him for longer, they've got to find some kind of evidence to pin on him, something substantial to make him a real suspect.

I have no doubt that these sleazy, shady FBI guys are more than willing to drum up some false information, any kind of fabricated evidence, just to make sure Leon doesn't wiggle out of their grasp. But I've been camped out here waiting all this time anyway. I'm too anxious to go home — and besides, where is home now, anyway? The hotel room I've only visited once to shower, rest, and change into the outfit I'm still wearing now? I might as well cancel that room and pick up all my belongings and live out of my rental car if I'm going to keep up like this.

As for my dad's old house? Well, it's not exactly a home if nobody's living there anymore, is it? His memory, his presence, still lingers like a shroud over the house. But that's not enough to make it a home again. So where would I go? If I'm being honest, I never even really felt at home back in the big city either. My little studio apartment was nice, filled with personal touches that made it feel a little less like renting a cardboard box. But it was lacking in memories. It was mostly just a crash pad and a writing space. Nothing particularly "homey" about that.

In fact, the closest thing to a home I've known in a long, long time is the comfort I found that night wrapped in Leon's arms. I felt protected there, pressed against his warm, hard body. I know it's gotta be one of the craziest things I've ever done, but something tells me I can't just walk away from this now, just because the water's gotten a little rough.

Leon saved me from drowning once, and I owe him. Besides, if he's the one who makes me feel like I'm finally home, then what kind of person would I be to walk away from that? If he's going to be stuck here in this musty old police station, then by God, I am gonna just camp out here, too.

And so I have.

The secretary gives me dirty, confused looks every now and again. I know she thinks

I'm straight-up insane for sticking around this long with no word from the cops about when Leon might be released. They won't give me any information at all. For all I know, they've already pinned all seventeen murders on him and they're taking their sweet time building an airtight — albeit false — case against him, and I'm waiting here for no reason.

But I can't take the chance that he'll be released and I won't be here.

I feel responsible, like I'm the one who dragged him into this. After all, it was *my* father's journal which led us to that field in the first place. I could have just left Leon out of it, investigated the case on my own. Or at least, I could have tried. But I know, deep down, he would have found his way into it, anyway. There's no chance he would have been able to keep out of it. He knew my father. He knows more about this whole mysterious, shady situation than I could ever know. I need his help. I need *him*.

So I wait, dutifully. Luckily I'm dressed in pretty comfortable clothes: a flowy gray blouse, dark jeans, and my most comfortable shoes, which are still kitten heels. That's definitely going to have to change pretty soon. I need to update my wardrobe to reflect the lifestyle I've fallen into back here in Bayonne. I'm not strutting Park Avenue anymore. I'm sneaking around warehouses, tromping through a field of unmarked graves, and riding on the back of a dangerous man's motorcycle.

It's probably high time for me to invest in a good pair of sneakers.

Good thing I'm always over-prepared. It's a trait of mine that my New York friends used to tease me for — the fact that my purse was always packed with anything I could possibly need in a pinch. Band-aids, breath mints, small pair of scissors, tape, mini sewing kit, always an extra toothbrush and travel-size toothpaste, face wipes, over-the-counter pain medication, an extra phone charger, and more. It's something I picked up during my long commutes back when I lived on Staten Island when I first moved out and couldn't afford to live in the city yet. When it takes you literally hours to get back home during an emergency, you start to realize how important it is to be mobile, to be prepared no matter how far you are from home.

So as I'm sitting in the police station, I've got my phone hooked up and charging so I can entertain myself and do some lowkey research. It's been an oddly productive activity, and I can't wait to share what I've learned with Leon. An hour ago I made a trek to the bathroom to brush my teeth and wash my face before returning to my little stakeout in the lobby. I'm prepared to live in this police station until they finally release Leon and the others. Secretarial shifts have changed multiple times, and each one of them has given me the same incredulous, somewhat-annoyed look. But now the girl who was working the desk when I first got here has returned again and she outright laughs when she walks in and sees me still here.

"We're gonna have to start charging you rent," she jokes as she swishes by to take her spot at the front desk. She's young and pretty, a brunette with round granny glasses and a pencil skirt. She looks more like a librarian than a cop jockey.

"Got more amenities than most of the apartments I could afford back in New York," I reply, shrugging. The secretary smiles.

"Are you hungry?" she asks. "Have you eaten anything since you first showed up?"

"Well, it depends on whether you consider vending machine snacks 'food' or not," I answer with a laugh, sitting up straight and setting my phone down to stretch my legs out.

She grimaces, wrinkling her nose. "Oh, ew. No, that won't do. I'll order us some sandwiches or something. At this point, you've been here more than I have in the past day or so, and at least I'm getting paid for it."

It's nice to see that my quiet persistence has won her over. Because even though I've been here forever, I haven't made a scene or caused any trouble — which is more than can be said for most of the people who probably come in here. So the secretary, who introduces herself as Janet, orders us both turkey subs from across the street. I scarf mine down in record time, realizing just how starved I am. We sit and joke back and forth with each other, passing the time until finally, at long last, an officer emerges with Leon in tow.

My heart leaps for joy in my chest and I can feel my whole body light up at the sight of him. When he sees me, his eyebrows shoot up in surprise and that adorable half-smile appears on his face. He looks so exhausted and burned out from hours and hours of interrogation, but I figure if they're bringing him out now, they must not have gotten what they were looking for. They are letting him go! He's free! For now, at least.

But something in his eyes tells me this isn't over yet, not by a long shot. Leon looks like he's seen and heard some terrible things in the past twenty-four hours or so. I want nothing more than to rush over to him and throw my arms around him. I want to kiss the sadness out of his face and take him back out into the sunshine. Except, I realize with a glance at the clock on the wall, the sun is already going down by now. Both of us have spent all our daylight hours cooped up in this station, though I expect his stay was considerably less comfy than mine.

"Leon!" I exclaim, despite the glumness of the moment. I need to make myself calm down — it's not like we're *together* or anything. It's not like that. But I can't seem to rid the thought from my head.

"Mr. Volkov is being released," the officer says gruffly. "Are you picking him up?"

"Oh — uh, yes!" I answer awkwardly, nodding. Leon gives me a grateful wink.

"At last the wait is over," Janet says, smiling at me. "It was nice to meet you."

"Thanks for putting up with me. And for the sandwich," I add.

"Now fill this out and go home and sleep, both of you," Janet replies, handing me a clipboard through the cut-out in the glass. I sign my name to check Leon out and then the officer takes off his cuffs and trudges away without a word. Leon turns to me and before he can say anything I wrap my arms around him and squeeze him tight.

His hand hesitantly comes down to pat my back and he rests his chin on my head for a long, still moment. "Don't tell me you waited this whole time," he murmurs.

I nod against his warm chest. "Yeah. It wasn't so bad. And I — I didn't want to leave you."

"I should have known they'd hold me as long as they legally could," he replies, shaking his head with restrained fury. "As if I would actually tell them anything."

"Come on," I say, taking him by the hand. I scoop all my stuff back into my bag and lead Leon out into the fresh air. We both take deep breaths, looking up at the late sunset.

"How was it?" I ask, a little reluctantly. I've never been interrogated, so I don't have any idea how they work. But if it's anything like it is on crime TV shows, it's definitely not a good time for anyone. Leon sighs heavily and puts an arm around me.

"Tiring. Boring, mostly. They asked me the same questions over and over with slightly different phrasing, as if that was going to trip me up. I knew exactly what they were doing the whole time. I've interrogated people before, myself. I know how it works. And they're just so… pompous. All of them. They don't even realize or care that I'm not the real bad guy here. They just want someone easy to pin shit on, and the Club is full of bright red targets," he says quietly, anger hardening his tone.

"This is bigger than any of the local police, isn't it?"

Leon nods and looks down at me. "Oh yeah. The FBI spooks just threw the local cops in there with me to keep all of us out of the way. They don't care about me or anyone from the Bayonne precinct at all. They just need to keep us occupied while they run their illicit operations all over town, so we can't do anything to stop them."

"But… I found out something," I say, biting my lip. "I looked into Agent Doyle's background. I mean, yeah, fashion blogging paid my bills but I've always been one hell of an investigator. Or just exceptionally, professionally nosy."

Leon laughs, the sound so welcoming and light. "And what did your research turn up?"

"He's way out of his league. Or at least his jurisdiction. He's not a homicide guy — he looks into stuff like tax evasion, corporate corruption, and other boring pencil-pusher things like that. There's no good reason for him to be here, taking over the investigation. He's not cut out for this stuff. He said this is FBI jurisdiction now — but if it's a mass homicide, why the hell would the feds send someone like *him* to clean it up?" I ramble all at once, tired of having to hold in this information for so long. I expect Leon to hug me, swing me around, and light up at this discovery. After all, what if this is the kick we need to take the case back from the feds and keep it a local issue?

But instead, Leon just squeezes my shoulder half-heartedly. "That's good work, Cherry. But unfortunately, these guys don't fold just because they've been caught counting cards. There's not a soul here we could report that to who would actually do anything about it. Even that Detective Hanson is useless against these guys. They're used to dealing dirty, and they aren't guided by a normal moral compass like we are. Hell, they don't even follow the law unless it serves their purposes. They're discriminatory enforcers, working in the shadows where nobody can follow, and for small-timers like us — they're damn near untouchable."

I feel my heart sinking and my cheeks burn with embarrassment. Here I thought I'd found something really good, something that would finally help us out, and it turns out I didn't find anything useful at all. What a letdown. I look down at the ground sadly.

"Oh. Damn."

"Yeah, it's hard. I know. But you can't give up just because the enemy is too big, alright? The Club has tangled with the feds before, and we came out of it relatively unscathed. Except for... you know, Henry. But that's the reason we can't give up. We fight for the ones who can't anymore, to remind those guys that we still remember what they did, and we refuse to let them off the hook for it. Any time we let them cow us with their scare tactics and threats, they get a little stronger. Even if they take us down, even when they win, we can't afford to retreat," Leon explains softly, kissing the top of my head.

"Why are they getting involved, anyway? The feds have never given a crap about Bayonne before," I mumble bitterly.

"Those incompetent local cops let something slip during the interrogation," Leon begins. "Turns out the reason the feds are here is because they're chummy with the crotchety old slimeball who owns the docks, Marty Chandler."

"So what the hell are we gonna do next?" I ask, feeling discouraged.

Leon shoots me a twinkling glance. "Well, first of all, we're gonna collect my bike from the impound lot. Then we're going somewhere."

"Where?" He takes my hand and starts pulling me along behind him.

"Somewhere. I have an idea."

CHAPTER 14 - LEON

"Leon, we're headed *away* from the docks, where are we going?"

"Not to the docks, obviously!"

Cherry gives me a punch on the arm, and I can hear her laughing over the roar of my engine as I speed us around a twisting road that leads through some woods and rocky ground. I've driven us south of the docks to a wooded area, guided by the moonlight alone.

After a few minutes more, Cherry settles down as she realizes we're moving upward and back around toward the water. Before long, I start slowing my bike down as we get close to the destination I have in mind.

There's a hilltop that overlooks the water, and with a tree clearing for tourists during the daytime, it offers a crystal-clear vantage point to the docks on the north side of the bay. We come to a stop, and I get out a pair of binoculars from the bike's seat compartment before leading Cherry towards the ledge.

"I remember this place," Cherry whispers, her eyes drinking in the scenery around her as walk. "I used to come here when I'd slip out at night as a teenager."

"You too?" I laugh. "I admit, I saw this place a lot more during the daytime. They uh, had a hard time keeping me in school when I was younger. This was a good place to come hang out on weekdays."

"Now look at you, you hoodlum," Cherry teases, nudging me with her elbow as we laugh quietly, careful not to risk drawing attention. "Anyway, this place is good, but there's somewhere a little higher up where we can see things even better."

Before I know it, she grabs me by the wrist and guides me off the trail a little ways. I follow, a smile on my face as we duck through some brush to climb up to a smaller hill that offers slightly better cover. I don't suspect anyone's going to give us trouble up here anyway, but this place feels more secluded.

I catch myself almost forgetting what we're here to do; I'm not a teenager out on a date, we're here to do some investigation. Running around with Cherry, though, it's easy to lose myself in the rush of things. She has a way of making me forget all the troubles that have been keeping us from really living for so long.

"Here," she says once we're in position, "this is the spot." We find a fallen log that I suspect people have been using here for a long time, and we take a seat to get comfortable.

For a while, the two of us just sit there, looking out over the still, cold waters and watching the moonlight cast a white path over its surface for miles and miles. I don't look over to see if her eyes are as transfixed on the sight as mine are. I can feel a peace between us that I can't really explain.

"Damn," I hear myself saying. "Everything is so still up here."

"Right?" Cherry says softly, leaning back and propping herself up by her hands. "The city almost looks kind of peaceful from here." That brings a smile to my lips.

It's funny, Cherry's reappearance in town should be just another hurdle to work through the storm of the past few days, but the more I think about it, the more I feel like she's at once an anchor and a motivation to keep going.

I finally glance over at her, and her eyes are on me. They look away quickly, but I keep mine on her. In the moonlight, her flowing gray blouse and tight dark jeans would almost make her meld into the wooded shadows if not for that flaming red hair of hers.

I try to raise the binoculars to my eyes, but I can't bring myself to focus on my target. For a few seconds, I even forget what the hell I'm supposed to be looking for out there, and my gaze just passes around the area listlessly.

I want her. I want to claim her.

The words in my mind are loud and clear, and I feel them welling up inside me like an irresistible storm. After every boss I've had to beat back, after every institution I've had to rebel against, after everything I've fought for, I've never felt a drive in me as strong as how much I want to bend Cherry LaBeau over the log we're sitting on and fuck her until she can't think of anything else. The feeling of her cunt around my manhood is still fresh in my mind, her breath on my neck, my hand on her ass.

She glances back and catches me gazing at her sidelong, and a smile plays across her face. "What's that look for?"

Her voice is playful, and so is my smile. "You're something else, Cherry."

She blinks and tilts her head to the side, those irresistibly glittering eyes of hers daring me to push a little further, ask a little more. "Oh yeah?"

"One second you're hiding out with the locals with me, the next minute you're accusing me of murder, and the next you're following me up to some mysterious hilltop to spy on goons in the moonlight."

One of her fingers is twirling around a lock of her crimson hair, and she finally lets the question I know she's been holding in all night spill out. "Is that really why you took me all the way up here, now?"

"Yeah," I say, my voice husky. "I don't think a self-respecting journalist would follow the most feared man in town around all week without a damn solid reason."

"Do I have a good reason?" she say in a near-whisper.

"You tell me," I growl, and my hand moves to her hip, the other sliding into her hair as I loom over her and press my lips hard against her.

Tonight, she's mine.

I'm at least a head taller than her, and she can feel it as I hug her tight into me, my hand gripping her sleeve as she lets out a stifled groan into my kiss, her arms wrapping around my rock-hard abdomen.

"What the fuck were you thinking," I growl between kisses as our lips part, "coming back into my life like this?"

"I was going to ask you the same thing," she says back, swinging one leg over the log and pulling herself further into me.

My hands are all over her, exploring her body voraciously, and hers are fumbling across my muscles with as much desire, every second we'd spent together these past few days since the last time we fucked spilling over. We're finally alone. Finally uninhibited. And I'm not going to waste a second of it.

Our seat becomes inconvenient, so I slide a knee to the ground, pulling her down with me and holding her up over me to cushion the fall. She nearly collapses atop me, and she just lets out a whimper of desire as I pull her close into me again, my hands grabbing her ass hard as I grind up against her.

My mouth is at her neck, sucking at the sensitive flesh with renewed energy. My hardened cock bulges in my pants, desperate to get out. Desperate for Cherry.

It doesn't take long for me to work her blouse off, and as it falls to the ground, her fingers are already fumbling to unhook her bra for fear that I'd rip the damn thing off. She can sense my hunger for her, and all she wants is to goad it on — to be utterly taken.

Her bra falls aside and her breasts spill out. In an instant, I sit up, sliding my jacket off, and I have to work my t-shirt off between her groping at me desperately. I toss the jacket and the shirt to the ground and push Cherry onto it, using it to pad her against the dirt. It might be disrespectful to the patch, but to me, she's worth it. And the only one who'd dare question me over it is putting her lips to my neck, wrapping herself around me.

She's already kicked off her shoes, and I work her pants down with ease, her hips twisting to help get them off faster. She's not wearing underwear. A grin spreads across my face as she lets herself lie there, totally exposed to me, practically panting for me to pierce her.

"Not yet," I say, "I've got something else in mind for you."

I bring my face down to her waiting, needy cunt and drag my tongue across her slit, slow and deep, and she lets out a long moan as her hands grip my head, getting a fistful of my hair as she presses herself up into me. Her taste is strong and it's driving me fucking wild.

My tongue wastes no time in starting to stroke her rhythmically, and Cherry is gasping with each stroke. The stubble of my beard brushes against her skin as I move up and down, the tip of my tongue venturing deep inside her before playing around the outer edges of her pussy. I can feel her insides electrifying at its touch, her muscles tightening and her hips twitching as I explore her. Then my tongue moves up to her clit, and her knees jerk up as it strikes it relentlessly, swirling around the sensitive spot at the crown of her cunt.

I feel her legs wrap around me as I work with machine-like rhythm and animalistic vigor. "Fuck, don't stop, Leon," she begs me, "God, what even are you?"

I don't answer, but get bolder and more intrusive with my mouth, stroking deep and ending at her clit each time. With every stroke, she anticipates it, but like a rolling inevitability, she nearly seizes up as I hit the golden spot. I start to feel her muscles tightening, faster and faster, but just as she starts to grip my sides hard, I withdraw, and her eyes spring open from the trance I've stroked her into. She looks almost hurt, wounded that I'd deny her, but as I undo my jeans and let them slide down, her pain turns to renewed lust at the sight of my cock.

Gripping her hips with my hands, I first pull her towards me and lunge forward to bite at her neck. She lets out a gasp as my teeth graze her skin, my fingernails running down her back as I suck at the nape of her neck relentlessly, meaning to leave a mark. Her squirming relaxes almost immediately, and she turns her head away to expose herself to me, inviting my assault, begging me to claim her.

I finally draw back and let her look up into me, looming over her and glaring into her eyes with unmitigated desire. For the briefest instant, I remember why we're here, and the next, I toss the thought aside. Nothing will stand between us tonight.

That's the liberty in my mind as I start to grind the tip of my cock into her, swirling it around her clit as she pushes herself up into me while I support her neck with one hand. "Turn around," I say in a husk as I guide her hips, and she obeys, turning over to present her ass to me while she supports herself on my kutte.

"Do you want this?" I ask, pressing my bulging, dark crown against her lips from behind, and even that simple motion has her pressing herself back into me, but I hold her hips firm. "I want to hear it."

"God, Leon, *please,*" she whimpers, "fill me up, I want all of you inside me!"

Without another word, I impale her with my cock from behind, and my crown crashes against that most sensitive spot inside her, and she nearly crumples to the ground under me as her honey floods my shaft. She tries not to yell out in ecstasy as I start bucking into her with abandon, and her teeth sink into the collar of my kutte as my hips work.

My cock pumps her like a piston, back and forth without missing a beat on each assault on the insides of her cunt. Her tightness is ecstasy for me. We share our warmth, and even as I claim her on the ground, I feel a closeness with her I've never felt before.

I pound into her furiously, her soft ass pressing into my pelvis as I go, and I have no plans to be cautious. I release all my inhibitions on her, and soon, I feel her cunt tightening even further around my manhood as she takes a sharp breath.

Then she lets out a piercing groan into my kutte as her orgasm bursts through her body, wracking her from her torso to her legs as I hold her up to keep her from falling over under me. I keep my pace, and I can feel her jerking and twisting under me as more waves of pleasure flow through her unimpeded as I keep my piston-like rhythm.

I feel my balls start to tighten as they slap against her wet cunt, and my fierce bucking starts to lose its regularity as my cock stiffens harder and harder, swelling up inside her.

"Don't hold back!" I hear her beg as she feels what's coming, "Come inside me, Leo — "

Her word is cut off as she lets out a yelp and I release myself in her with a deep, husky groan, all the tension I've been holding back unleashing itself all over her insides. Long, hard shots of myself shoot up into her as I come, each one with a hard throb that makes her twitch each time.

I pull out of her, and the hot, pearly fluid spills out with me, the silence of the night accented by our heavy, exhausted breathing. Cherry turns over to look at me, shirtless and looming with my cock still stiff and wet with her honey, and a smile makes its way through her panting.

"So, strictly business tonight, right?"

I can't hold back a deep chuckle, and I slap her on the thigh as she scurries up to get herself dressed again.

*****

We've cleaned ourselves up, and half an hour later, the night has descended into staring at the docks through the pair of binoculars I'd nearly forgotten beside me. We hand it to each other from time to time, trying to scope out anything of value, but it isn't until around midnight that something catches my eye.

"Why didn't I notice *that* before?" I murmur to myself, and Cherry cranes her neck to try to see what I'm looking at, resting her hands on my shoulders and leaning on my back.

"Well, what is it?"

"That ship down there, I see someone moving around on it."

"So? Have you not been seeing the people milling around? They're shady old docks, that happens from time to time."

"Yeah, but this one in particular. I can see the name on the side of the ship. It's the *Canary*

Islander. That ship hasn't been in use in...well, years. It was deemed unseaworthy back before the union was busted. Yeah, I can see at least three people down there."

I hand Cherry the binoculars, and she nods after peering through them for a few moments. "You're right. Recognize anyone down there?"

"No — and that's what worries me," I say, squaring my jaw thoughtfully for a second. "I don't like this. Come on," I say, standing up and stowing the binoculars.

"What, are we just gonna leave now?"

"Naw, where's your investigative spirit?" I say, giving a cocky grin as I pull my kutte back on and start walking towards the bike. "We're gonna go pay them a visit *right now*."

Cherry looks hesitant for a moment, but as I give a nod for her to follow me to my bike, she steps forward, picking up her shoes and heading after me.

"Good thing I think you know what you're doing," she half-laughs.

"That's my girl," I say as she clambers onto the back of the bike. As I rev up the engine, I feel her slip her hands around my waist as she considers what I'd just said.

"I think I like the sound of that."

CHAPTER 15 - CHERRY

The back streets leading up to the coast are only dimly lit by the moon's eerie glow as we park the motorbike and start walking. There are lamp posts here and there, but most of them have long burned out, never to be replaced by the public officials who regard this area of town as a sort of lost cause. And the bulbs that remain with just a spark of life only flicker weakly, lending less light and more ominous atmosphere to our nocturnal mission.

We parked a few blocks away just off the road because the motorcycle engine is not exactly stealthy — you can hear it coming from miles away. Anyway, this time of night there aren't a whole lot of vehicles or people passing through this area, so we'd stand out even in my much quieter rental. Not to mention the fact that both the local cops and the feds will definitely keep an eye out for motorcyclists at this point. They know we're onto them, and if they're smart they also know that we won't give up just because they rattled the Club up a little bit with those interrogations. And we can't risk blowing our cover, not tonight.

We're going in to check out the abandoned docks where we heard suspicious sounds earlier, to find out what the hell could possibly be going on there. I mean, they *are* abandoned, so nothing should be going on there at all.

Leon and I are walking softly, keeping close together, our eyes peeled, searching for any hints of danger or discovery. I feel like I'm still glowing from our moonlit tryst earlier, but I try to keep my head calm despite the giddy butterflies flitting around in my stomach. It's ridiculous how even in a high-stakes, gritty situation like this I am still so distracted by how much I like Leon. How intensely his touch affects me.

He makes me come alive like nothing else does.

And he takes me to places I've never been — even though we're physically in the same town we both grew up in. It's so strange to me how new and unfamiliar my hometown is when I'm traipsing through it with Leon. He gives me a new perspective on everything, showing me both the dark, terrifying underbelly of the city and the passionate, defiant camaraderie of those who fight against it. It's just like a movie, and he's the star.

Which might just make me the love interest.

Well, if that's the case, I sure as hell hope I'm not a damsel in distress. I don't feel like one, not anymore. At Leon's side I feel powerful, like an electric current is buzzing through my veins and heightening my senses. With one simple touch of his hand, I transform into a spy, a secret agent, an action heroine. I love it.

Gone is the Cherry LaBeau of New York City, the girl who holed up in her loft and dashed off shallow, insignificant gossip and fashion articles for a paycheck. Gone is the high-maintenance, high-life, high-rise Park Avenue princess who was afraid to get her hands dirty. I don't resent that girl, and I know deep down she will always be a part of me, and I will look back fondly on those years I spent prancing through the Big Apple without a care in the world. But now there's a new Cherry, and she's one tough broad. She can run with the wolves. She fights for what's right, even when it's hard. She isn't afraid of getting down in the mud and getting filthy when need be.

I like the new Cherry a lot. I think I'm gonna keep her.

"Shh, look," Leon whispers, holding out his arm to halt me, then pointing up ahead a ways. I squint in the darkness to make out the movements of several black vehicles, glinting ever so subtly in the moonlight. Black sedans. The feds are here.

But that's not all… there are several vans, too. Gray, nondescript, unmarked vans. They look for all the world to be exactly the kind of van your parents tell you to avoid as a kid.

"Let's go closer," I murmur softly. Leon shoots me an impressed look, then nods in agreement. He takes my hand and a thrill passes down my spine as he leads me onward, the two of us creeping along in the shadows of the trees and telephone poles.

As we sneak slowly and carefully closer, I'm able to make out something huge moving laboriously on the water, with long, tall beams. Leon stops me again and nudges me further off the sidewalk into a clump of brush across the street from the parking lot to the docks.

"Is that the ship?" I ask in an undertone, my heart racing. I still don't know why in the world would there be a ship coming into the abandoned docks, but I know it can't be for anything legal.

"Yeah. I guess it's actually running somehow."

"Don't they have to, like, register that or something? You can't just drive a big-ass boat up anywhere willy-nilly," I hiss. Leon shakes his head and narrows his eyes, straining to look at the bizarre scene unfolding in front of us.

"See those big, black cars? That's all the legality they need. A couple of feds to pave the way and keep the public out of their business, and even the nastiest crime boss can get his work done right under the citizens' noses," he replies quietly, clenching his jaw tightly.

Then I see something even stranger. It looks like the ship is pulling in and starting to unload a series of massive, heavy-duty containers, big enough to hide elephants inside.

"What the hell?" I mumble. Leon squeezes my hand.

"Come on," he urges, "let's go closer. If that's what I think it is…"

His voice trails off as he pulls me along behind him. We both crouch as we bolt across the road and into the parking lot. I'm grateful that we're both dressed in pretty dark clothing, so we don't stand out too much in the shadowy lot. Either way, there's not a whole lot to hide behind here, so this leg of the journey is considerably riskier. If any of those people on the docks just happen to turn around and look directly our way, they'd catch us. My heart is pounding, but somehow I still feel relatively calm. Leon makes me feel safe, even in the most dangerous of situations. We're still a few hundred yards from where the black cars and creepy vans are parked, but I know we are essentially inside the lair of the beast right now.

There's a dilapidated old green dumpster nearby, and Leon pulls me beside him several yards to hide behind it. I try not to gag at the musty smell, deciding it will be better for now to just… breathe through my mouth. But at least we have some kind of cover here, and we can still poke our heads around the side of the dumpster to watch what's happening on the docks.

The vans are driving up close to where the ship has pulled in to a stop. Feds in black suits and sketchy workers in black hoodies and baseball caps stand on the docks awaiting the containers to be unloaded. I watch with bated breath as the first of these giant boxes is opened.

And my jaw drops.

I was afraid it would be filled with weapons or drugs or something. But what I see now is so much worse. Filing slowly out of the container is a huddled mass of human beings, trudging out and dragging their feet. They all look exhausted, their heads hanging and their bodies thin, dressed in ripped, stained rags. They've got to be immigrants, being shuffled into Bayonne for what? Hard labor? Servitude?

"Oh my God," I breathe, starting to shiver.

Leon's chest is heaving, breathing hard. I glance up at him to see the mingled horror, fury, and despair on his handsome face. His hands are balled into fists and he looks like he might run down to the docks and start swinging at any moment.

"It's exactly what I feared," he murmurs, swiping one huge hand down his face.

"Who are they? Where did they come from?" I question, tears tingling in my eyes at the sight of their bare feet and battered limbs. Some of the women are crying, and the men have distant, far-away looks on their faces.

"From all over, I'm sure. Wherever the price of human life is cheapest," Leon snarls.

There are multiple containers, at least three from what I can tell. And sure enough, all of them are opened to reveal similarly-disheveled, malnourished, world-weary people inside. The men in suits stand by, emotionless with their hands behind their backs or crossed on their chests, like they're simply statues-for-hire planted strategically along the docks to guard this illicit deal. And the men in hoodies guide the miserable people down the docks and into the backs of the vans. It's a horrifying sight. I know they aren't bringing these people here to give them a chance at a better life. They aren't rescuing them. They're herding them like cattle.

Probably to be used much like cattle. Used up and tossed aside.

I tear my eyes away from this heartbreaking procession to land on another sight which chills me to the bone. There are two men overlooking the whole thing with nonchalance, one of them smirking and gesturing jovially to the other. One is in a sleek black suit and tie — and I recognize him after a moment of squinting and wracking my brain.

Agent Doyle. Of course that bastard is involved.

And beside him, talking and joking with gleeful abandon, is an old, potbellied man in a tacky white suit and red tie. He oozes wealth, the kind of exorbitant, obnoxious wealth that indicates he has no intention of spending his money responsibly. He looks like the epitome of greed and selfishness, like a pig in a silk jacket and a salt-and-pepper toupee.

"Who's that talking to Doyle?" I whisper. Leon sighs.

"Martin Chandler, the rich douchebag who owns the docks. He's like a festering sore on this town, draining all the resources and sucking the life out of the working folk," Leon answers with a grimace.

"Leon, what is going on here?" I ask fearfully, turning to him.

He bites his lip and puts a hand on my shoulder. "You wouldn't want to know."

"Tell me, I can take it."

"Cherry, I — "

Just then, he's interrupted by a loud voice down near the docks.

A man shouts out: "Hey! Over there!" Everyone turns to look toward where the man is pointing: directly at us. We've been spotted.

"Shit," Leon whispers, grabbing me so we can both duck back behind the dumpster.

One second later, there's the deafening crack of several gunshots.

CHAPTER 16 - LEON

The metal container to my left rings sharply as a bullet ricochets off it. I grab Cherry by the collar as I yank her down and curse. My hand instinctively goes to the handgun at my side and cock it as more bullets whiz over our heads.

"Back to the bike," I growl, "keep low and close to me!"

Cherry's gives a sharp nod, and her reflexes prove sharper than I realized as she keeps neck-and-neck with me as we duck out from our hiding spot and start weaving between the large metal containers, the sounds of gunfire behind us echoing throughout the docks.

We near the opening on the other side of the 'alley' we're running through when a barrel-chested man steps out in front of us, raising his pistol. I raise my gun in response, but before either of us can get a shot out, a bright LED light shines in his face — Cherry is holding her flashlight up straight in his eyes. "Shit!" He shouts and puts a hand up and tries to move for cover, but I'm already on him, and my fist connects with the side of his head hard before he hits the ground with a thud.

Once we're out, we crouch down and move through what feels like a maze of metal canisters set out to be loaded and shipped. I can hear Doyle's voice shouting out across the docks. "I don't *care* who it might be, find them and get them before I have *your* asses packed away with the next shipment!"

"They don't know it's us," Cherry hisses to me, and I give a sharp nod. I intend to keep it that way.

A few men were drawn to where I dropped the man who yelled, so I know we only have a few seconds before they turn their attention our way. I grab Cherry's hand and dart towards where I left my bike.

My motions are quick, decisive, and without a hint of hesitation. Cherry is surprisingly adept at being able to keep up, but my sudden changes in direction start to throw her after a while.

"Are you used to this kind of thing?" she whispers.

"You'd be surprised," I say back in a low voice. I knew my background would always be there to haunt me as I try to lead an honest life, but never did I think I'd see the day that my past as a hitman would come to serve me like this. Yet the pistol in my hand feels no heavier than the last time I'd used it.

Finally, the bike comes into view as we crouch behind a stack of crates. But there's a lot of open ground to there, and I get a bad feeling.

"Wait here," I say to Cherry, "I'll drive it over and pick you up. This will need to be smooth and quick." Before she can respond, wide-eyed, I press my lips to hers before I pull out a bandana from my jacket and wrap it around my face and ready my pistol as I run out for my bike.

I'm nearly to it when I hear a voice shout out from behind me.

"FREEZE!"

I whip around instinctively and find myself facing off with another thug, a face from out of town I don't recognize. On the bright side, he won't recognize me, either.

"Drop the gun, I won't say it twice."

"Do what he says," orders a second voice from behind me, and my grip tightens. I'm surrounded, and I hear the click of a pistol from the second assailant as well.

I ready myself. I'm not about to back down, so my muscles tense as I prepare to shoot and move quickly, praying the next thing I know isn't a bullet in the back.

"You deaf? Gun on the ground, hands up, or I shoot!" the first man orders, and when I don't immediately respond, I see him aim his pistol to fire his weapon.

Then there's a *crack* from behind me, and I glance back just in time to see Cherry, having brought a lead pipe down on the second man's head, now diving to grab his gun as the thug falls to the ground.

I look back to see the first man taken off-guard just long enough, and without a second thought I fire a shot into the man's shoulder, and he staggers back, gun falling from his hands as he lets out a sharp yell.

I close the distance between us, and as his murderous eyes turn to me, he hurls a punch to my gut, but I catch it with my free hand. He blinks in surprise, and that's the last thing he has time to do as I bring my forehead crashing down on his nose, knocking him out cold.

"Let's go!" I shout at Cherry, and in no more than two seconds we've sprinted to the bike. I'm revving up the engine before roaring down the street as more cries of alarm shout out from behind us.

Cherry's arms wrap around me tight as we ride. "You did good," I say back to her, grin on my face.

"We're not out of the woods yet," she warns, glancing back at the headlights behind us. One of the black sedans from the docks is deciding to chase us.

I laugh. "If these tourists want to go for a ride, I'll play ball."

Gunshots ring out from the sedan almost immediately, but I've already started weaving on my bike. It's hard enough to shoot from a moving vehicle, much more so at a moving target.

I drive up the docks and towards the city, wondering whether they'll have the stones to follow me into the streets proper. Either way, I don't want the police to get involved in the chase, so I decide it's time to end things early. Without warning, I veer off my path and come screeching to a halt just as the sedan gains on us.

It goes zooming past, to the astonishment of the men inside, and before they can react, I aim a couple of shots at their back tires. After the shots ring out, I hear the car screeching as the tires go out. They careen to the side of the road, and before they know what's happened, I'm roaring past them and into the city streets, Cherry looking back on the scene with wide eyes as I feel her heart pounding against my back.

*****

To be safe, I take us on a ride through the back alleys of the city again, not unlike what I did to give the police the runaround last time. With these men, though, I'm more confident they won't dare drag this into the city proper.

"...with Agent Doyle at the helm of that, I'm sure someone's been paid to turn a blind eye to the cops for the night," I explain to Cherry, "but take things into citizens' front yards, and they wouldn't have a choice. We'll wait for things to cool off at the Glass."

A few minutes later, we make the roundabout and pull up at our bar. It feels like it's been hours, but it's not even 1:00 AM yet, and it looks like most of the club has been hanging around the bar, worried about why I haven't at least checked in yet.

As I push the door open, Cherry at my side, I see the whole club gathered together.

Genn and Eva are playing pool in the corner, and they raise their beers to me as soon as we enter.

"Hey, Prez! Heard gunshots, glad to see you both in one piece."

"Genn was just waiting on you to watch the table so I don't cheat while he takes a piss."

"Shaddup!"

Eva elbows Genn in the side as we stride in, and I hear more greetings from the club.

"Got any dirt on the feds, Prez?" Anya asks after she downs the remainder of her vodka. "With all Doyle's goons crawling around, I'm getting kind of impatient patching people up, starting to think I was born to crack heads instead."

"Shoulda been with us today," I chuckle back at her, pulling away my bandana to show off the cut on my forehead where I headbutted one of the thugs. "Got a little closer to the old days than I'd like to admit."

Now I've really got the bar's attention.

"Tell us you've got something solid, Prez," Vasily asks, rubbing his sore bicep after losing an arm wrestling match with Roy, one of the grizzled older members. Given how many beers there are around the table, I figure it's their sixth or seventh match. "I want to work out these arms on a little more than letting Roy win a few times."

"You gonna be six beers in when you 'let them win' too, kid?" Roy laughs, and Vasily waves him off with a curse in Russian.

"I think we do have something, in fact," comes Cherry's voice, to my surprise. I give her my attention with a nod, standing back to let her speak, and after my example, the rest of the bar gathers around to listen up. Cherry looks a little taken aback by the deference, but she clears her throat and continues.

"Right. So Agent Doyle and his lackeys are down at the docks, right now. What's worse, he's got what looks like muscle from out of town helping him. They're working out of an old ship that should have been scrapped years ago, and now we know why — they're shipping *people* in that tin can. Packing them in like sardines."

There's a grumble throughout the bar, and I can practically hear people gripping their beers tighter. A few of the immigrants among us are first or second-generation Russians like me, and some of them have very personal experiences with the human traffickers in New York.

"Looks like most of them come from south of the border. We saw Doyle coordinating with Marty Chandler down there. The dock owner is in on whatever operation's going on down there. I don't think it's a long shot to guess those victims we found buried in the field are some of the men and women who didn't survive the journey."

"Sons of bitches," I hear Eva hiss in the background.

"And it makes sense now," Cherry goes on, pacing around the bar. "If Doyle keeps us distracted with him while they push through the sale of that empty lot, the secret gets buried for good the moment a NexaCo gets built on top of those graves."

It feels like there's a pall over the whole club. Genn spits on the ground in disgust, and Roy looks about ready to storm out the bar and start raising hell that second. Most of the older members look to be of the same mind.

"I'm tired of these goddamn feds walking all over us with a free pass to do whatever the fuck they want!" Anya shouts, slamming a fist down on the table as she sways in her seat. Vasily nods to her in agreement, cracking his knuckles.

"We can pound our chests all we like," Genn says glumly, "but it's the FBI. We can't lay a finger on Doyle, and the chickenshit knows it. And if we can't touch Doyle, we can't touch his buddies, either. As far as they're concerned, they're golden."

"That's why they've been so bold," Eva adds on. "Marty Chandler's friends aren't just taking advantage of the FBI's presence, they *know* he'll save their asses when they start pulling off shit we'd bust their heads open for."

Cherry crosses her arms and chews on her lip, thinking, but after a few moments, she looks to me, a concerned look on her features. "I don't know. What's your take...Prez?"

Hands on my hips, I think for a moment, brow furrowed, but when I open my mouth to speak, someone calls me to the door behind me. When I turn and head out the door to see who's there, the ghost of Joe Hill himself couldn't have shocked me more.

"The Lone Wolf," I say darkly to Mikhail. "You've got some fucking nerve coming back into this town." Of all the people in the world I expected to see in the club's parking lot, he was right around the bottom of the list.

The man standing by the car is every bit as tall and muscular as I am, with slightly darker hair and a clean-shaven face. A designer jacket hangs on his shoulders, unadorned with any patches or markings of any kind. He's almost the spitting image of myself, but more clean-cut, his Russian heritage as plain as day. I send a message with my kutte. He sends a message with his eyes.

I raise my fist to him playfully, and he goes for my ribs before we break into laughter.

"Leon! You are quicker than ever," Mikhail says with a smile.

"Quick enough to put a fright into your Old Woman," I say, shooting a half-smirk over towards the woman waiting by the car who'd just squeaked like a frightened mouse. Where'd she think he was taking her to that an honest fight would break out right away? "My most sincere apologies, ma'am," I grin, laying on the charm.

"I was just playing the role of the audience," the pretty, young woman says back. She's quick witted at least, even if she does seem shaken up.

"Sorry my timid *kotika,*" Mikhail says, releasing me and stepping around the car to extend his hand to his woman. "Come meet Leon. Leon, this is Alicia," he says. He puts his arm around her, laying his claim as clear as day. Never thought I'd see Mikhail of all people takin' a shine to someone like this.

"Ahh, she is indeed a pussycat," I grin, and for Mikhail's benefit, I take her hand, kissing her knuckles. "Welcome to Bayonne, Alicia."

I'm trying to stay calm, but I know if Mikhail is here, trouble is following him, and trouble is the last thing we need. Not with the feds, not with these slimeballs trying to take over our city and bringing in human slaves.

But I can't say no to him. Not after all we've been through. Even if he is bringing the heat down on us.

"Now hands off of her," Mikhail says, pushing away my arm before we head on inside. A few of them grin and cheer excitedly for Mikhail's return, knowing who he is to me and what he once meant to the area.

"Some people you know?" Cherry asks, stepping close to my side as the man steps in and looks at me with the same familiar recognition that's on my face.

"Yeah," I chuckle, "it's been a hell of a long time, but I like to think I know him. He's the walking, talking reminder of my past, in more ways than one, but dammit, he's family."

Cherry's eyes widen. "You mean…"

"Yeah," I reply, stepping forward to give Mikhail a tight hug. "This towering giant is my brother, both by blood and by the Bratva" I say, looking back at Cherry with a rugged smile.

CHAPTER 17 - CHERRY

I look back and forth between the two of them with my mouth hanging wide open. How could they possibly be related? *Brothers*? Leon and Mikhail are both stunningly handsome and undeniably Russian, but otherwise so different. Leon looks like a pretty typical — albeit hunkier than usual — working class guy, with his mischievous smile and lowkey style. But Mikhail looks like a mobster. Like an emotionless killing machine.

"Mikhail, let me introduce to you to my girl. This is Cherry LaBeau," Leon says, reaching out and taking my hand. He releases his brother and stands next to me, beaming. He looks like an excitable puppy showing me off to his big brother, and the fact that he called me his girl is making my head spin with delight.

Mikhail is tall and straight-backed, his bearing regal and intimidating. He's dressed in all black, his clothing neatly pressed and immaculately tailored to his muscular body. By comparison, Leon is much more relaxed and Americanized. Even though I can still sense that Russian resilience and power in him, but Leon smiles and laughs more easily. I get the feeling that Mikhail doesn't do either of those things very often. Maybe ever.

He holds out his hand to shake mine. I oblige him quickly, my eyes wide as I look up into his stony face. "*Ochyen priyatno, sestra*. It's a pleasure."

"Same here," I reply nervously, giving him a weak smile. He scares the pants off of me.

Then he immediately turns back to Leon and leans in to murmur, "*Moy brat*, I have a favor to request of you."

Leon puts an arm around me and grins at his brother. "Anything for you."

Mikhail glances around the room at everyone. Half the people are pretending not to pay attention, and the other half are just outright staring. *Way to play it cool, guys,* I think to myself bemusedly. Leon notices the same thing and rolls his eyes.

"Uh, let's go in the back and discuss this, eh?" he suggests. Mikhail nods.

At first I assume they're going to head into the back office without me, as I'm probably not exactly at the high level of security clearance required for whatever mafia-esque business Mikhail could possibly want to discuss. But Leon pulls me by the hand behind him, the four of us passing through a wide berth in the crowd. Everyone seems to move out of Mikhail's way. I wonder if it's just his ominous presence that does it, or if he has some kind of dark reputation preceding him.

When we get to the back and Leon closes the door behind us, he turns back and asks his brother, "So, what is it? What do you need?"

Mikhail replies grimly, "I need you to help me hide Alicia, *bratishka.*" I can tell from the way Mikhail says her name that she's the one he loves. It's hard to imagine such a tight-lipped, buttoned-up statue of a man having tender feelings for anyone, but there it is. And it's obvious by the genuine concern clouding his face that he'd do anything to keep her safe. "A few months should do the trick. Then I'll come back and see she's sent along safely."

Instantly I can tell that Alicia is crushed, and my heart hurts for her. Didn't Mikhail discuss this with her? She looks way too shocked for that.

"You'll come back?" She asks, but Mikhail doesn't look at her. He's forcing his hard gaze on Leon, but I can see the flicker of anguish pass his features.

"Mikhail, I don't know if we can do that right now," Leon says sadly, shaking his head. I can tell it pains him greatly to disappoint his brother. "The FBI is on our backs, brother, and there's not a single place in this town we could hide her without them sniffing her out. It just isn't safe here in Bayonne. It's not like it used to be when we were boys."

"*Pozhaluysta*. I beg of you," the older brother answers, a pleading edge to his tone.

"What happened to the usual safe houses?" Leon asks, frowning.

Mikhail looks aside as though embarrassed. "They've been... compromised."

"What? How did that — " Leon stops abruptly, seeing the authentic sadness on his brother's face. I know the last thing he wants to do is let him down. I wonder what they were like growing up together as young boys and teenagers. I only saw Leon the one time at the beach, and I can't recall ever seeing Mikhail around. Then again, it's nearly impossible to imagine what this cold-blooded hitman would have looked like as an innocent child. The idea is almost laughable.

"I need to get her somewhere. She won't last in the city." The cold-hearted killer has a major weakness for the woman with him. And I can only imagine the trouble she's in. It doesn't seem like Mikhail has been back here in quite some time considering how Leon's acting.

Leon glances down at me beside him, and I wonder if he's thinking about me that way. If he's considering what he'd do in Mikhail's situation.

The two lovers that just arrived quibble. But it's the kind of quarrel that happens between two people who care for one another, when what's best for one isn't what's best for both. She doesn't want him to leave her, and I can't really blame her.

On the upside, their heated discussion gives Leon time to think.

When Alicia raises her hand to gently stroke Mikhail's cheek, Leon breaks the silent tension in the room. "I need your help, too. I think… maybe we can work out a deal."

Mikhail gives him a critical look and crosses his arms on his chest. "I will help you in any way I can. Whatever you need."

Leon takes a deep breath and then says flatly, "I need you to eliminate someone for me."

My mouth falls open again as my head whips around to look up at him in disbelief. Surely that can't mean what it sounds like. Leon is a tough guy who runs with a kind of dangerous crowd, I know, but he can't honestly be asking his brother to commit murder for him? Maybe it's some kind of code or something I just don't understand.

Mikhail doesn't react with the appropriate surprise or indignation at his brother's request. Instead, he just lifts his chin a little, narrowing his eyes and straightening his shoulders as though squaring up for a business deal. Like they're just talking about buying a car together—not killing somebody! He takes his chin in his huge, calloused hand and looks at Leon thoughtfully for a long moment. The silence is killing me and I almost want to jump up and down and wave my arms, shouting *'WHAT THE HELL?'*

But I don't.

Until finally I can't stand it anymore.

"Leon, what's going on? What do you mean, 'eliminate' someone?" I ask, my voice higher and more shrill than I hoped it would be. But under the circumstances, how could anyone expect me to keep a level tone, anyway?

Both brothers turn their eyes to me and I instantly feel my face start burning. They're both so intensely attractive and intimidating that I want to just shrink down into a ball and hide for even daring to interrupt this discussion. Alicia just looks at me with a mixture of pity and envy.

I half expect Leon to kick the two of us out of the office so the men can continue their talk in private. But I should know by now that he's better than that—he's not like the snobby, dismissive, condescending guys I sometimes had to contend with at work back in the city. Those guys looked down on me for my name, my looks, my girly journalism. As if their boring sports articles were any more world-changing than my fashion pieces, anyway.

Alicia disentangles herself from Mikhail and sits in one of the nearby chairs, her face distant as though she's in a trance, but I can't worry about that now. Right now, I need to worry about the fact that my boyfriend is asking his brother to murder someone in cold blood.

But Leon just places a gentle hand on my back and gives me a sympathetic, meaningful look.

"Cherry, if this is getting to be too much, I won't hold it against you if you want to take a step back. I don't want you to be in any danger, and I don't want to force you into anything you don't feel comfortable with. I promise I will do anything and everything in my power to keep you safe from harm or retribution, but I will warn you that this is dangerous territory we're going into now. It's always been this way, and I'm in too deep to dig my way out. But it's not too late for you to back out if that's what you want. I won't stop you. I just want you to be okay," Leon explains, his voice so patient and gentle.

I stand there blinking dumbly for a moment while I try to sort through everything he just said. First of all, I am touched that he would feel such concern and tenderness for me. But second of all, I am slightly annoyed that he thinks I'm going to throw in the towel and run away at the first sign of real danger! I'd like to think I'm stronger than that, and I want him to know that I'm in this with him, for better or for worse.

After all, they're talking about the people who very well might have had a hand in my father's death.

"No," I tell him, shaking my head. "I'm gonna see this through. Even if it's scary. Even if I am definitely in over my head. I'm not leaving you and I'm not letting this go. I'm too invested. I have to find out what's going on here. It's—it's what my dad would have wanted me to do."

"*Smelaya devushka,*" Mikhail comments. I turn to see him smiling down at me, a hint of pride in his face. He gives Leon a nod of approval before clapping me firmly on the shoulder.

"Brave girl, indeed," Leon murmurs, that devilish, delicious half-smile on his face again. Just knowing that I'm the one who's put that smile there is enough to make me feel all warm and tingly. Then he straightens up and continues, "If you're totally sure about this, then I need you to know that things may get a little… um, illegal, from here on out. To beat these bastards at their own game, we have to be just as cutthroat and willing to resort to drastic measures to get things done."

I nod, hardening my face and trying to look tough. "I understand. They fight dirty, so we have to get down in the mud with them."

"Exactly," Leon says, that smile trying desperately to appear again.

"But… still, isn't it a little too early to resort to murder?" I ask meekly, not wanting them to be angry with me. It feels like a legitimate concern, though, under the circumstances. Generally I think one should at least think twice before embarking upon a capital offense. In my personal opinion, flat-out murder should probably be Plan Z, not Plan B.

"I respect and understand your hesitation," Mikhail says cautiously. "Your concern for human life is refreshing. But we do not extinguish lives for the thrill, and we only do so when it is to the greater benefit of the majority."

Nodding, Leon adds, "And this particular target is nothing but a pustule on the face of the planet. He's not worth the oxygen he's been slurping up for decades. His existence has directly resulted in the deaths of many, many innocent people. He is not deserving of your concern, nor your pity, Cherry."

It's a little chilling to hear him speak this way, so intensely and darkly. He talks about taking a life with a tone of resignation. He is thoroughly certain that what he feels is right. And I don't know enough about the subject to truly disagree with him. Of course, I have always been a pacifist, almost to a fault. I flee from confrontation and avoid conflict of any kind like the plague. But then, that's part of why I've been stuck writing innocuous puff pieces for so long.

When the world sees that you're not willing to fight, it tends to write you off.

Well, I'm ready to fight now, even if I'm not sure what will come of it.

"Who is it? The target, I mean?" I question, looking back and forth between them.

"That was going to be my next question, too," Mikhail says.

"Brother, I need you to take out Martin Chandler," Leon replies, with an air of finality.

I feel sick to my stomach immediately. There is no possible way this will turn out well. From what I've gleaned about him, Marty Chandler is far too well-known and well-connected to be quietly taken care of. I'm sure he has the strongest security team Bayonne's ever seen, and his death will certainly not go unnoticed, if it even gets that far.

"M-Martin Chandler?" I repeat, a little breathlessly. "Isn't he that guy from the docks? The rich guy talking to Agent Doyle? How the hell are you going to get rid of him? Won't people *notice*?"

Mikhail laughs, a deep and throaty sound which actually startles me and makes me jump slightly.

"I'm no amateur," he assures me. "I have killed many men much more powerful and influential than that sewer slime Chandler. And so has my brother."

I look back to Leon nervously. I should have known that. It should not come as a surprise. But somehow, I still find myself a little frightened… and strangely, inexplicably aroused.

What is *wrong* with me?

It's just reassuring, I suppose, to hang around someone who would probably, definitely kill for me if need be. Especially because I have caught glimpses of his heart even in the short time I have spent with him, and I know his intentions to be good and true.

He's not a bad man; he's a very, very good man who sometimes resorts to very, very bad things.

And after what he's seen… I can't say I really blame him.

"I hope that doesn't frighten you away," Leon says to me softly, and I can tell he is genuinely worried that it might. I wonder how many women have fallen for his looks and daring personality, only to run away from his troubled past and dangerous lifestyle. I want to prove to him that I can take it. I want to show him I'm strong enough to stick around, even if it gets rough.

Because I'm starting to fall for him.

"It probably should," I mumble, meeting his gaze a little reluctantly. His bright green eyes are mesmerizing in their sadness. "But it won't. I'm not going anywhere."

"Then it's settled," Mikhail cuts in, rubbing his hands together.

"And once Chandler is taken care of, that will solve at least a few of our problems. It will throw off the feds' operation for awhile, just long enough for us to infiltrate and put a stop to it. Without Chandler around, Agent Doyle won't have easy access to the abandoned docks, so he will have to find a new way to hustle his huddled masses into town," Leon explains. Then he adds, "Besides, the bloody bastard deserves to die for what he's done."

"Agreed," Mikhail says simply.

"How will you do it?" I ask, unable to let it go. This is a whole new world for me, and even though I'm trying my best to remain calm, there's a voice screaming in the back of my head to run away and never look back. I try to silence it, but it remains. I suppose that must be the lingering shreds of my once sterling sense of self-preservation.

"Do not concern yourself with the details, *sestra*. Leave that to me. I have done this many times before, and I do not consider Martin Chandler a threat on any level," Mikhail assures me coolly.

"See? It will all be okay," Leon says, smiling. I can't believe this is happening, and I'm just going along with it. A week ago, if someone had told me I would be involved in this kind of ridiculous James Bond-esque situation, I would have laughed outright.

But things change. And here we are.

"And in return?" Mikhail presses, raising an eyebrow.

Leon turns back to him and gives him a nod. "I promise to find a safe place to hide

Alicia in the meantime. I have friends and connections all over town. Don't worry, *moy brat*."

"*Spasibo*, Leon."

The two of them shake hands and then embrace each other. I stand aside, smiling at them even though that voice in the back of my head is starting to get louder with every second that passes. Something tells me their plan is not as foolproof as they pretend it to be. I have this gnawing feeling in the pit of my stomach, warning me to run, run away. But I can't.

I'm already in.

CHAPTER 18 - LEON

"Don't worry about Alicia," I tell my brother as we head back out into the bar, "I know a club up in Jersey City who owe me a favor and have a safe house where I've personally lain low a few times. She'll be safe and comfortable. My vice-prez will take her there. Eva?"

She looks up from her pool game and strides over to us, giving Mikhail a nod as she does.

"Got anything going on tomorrow?"

"Nah, I can tell my techs to handle things 'till the afternoon." Eva owns a mechanic shop not far from here.

"Good. Do that — I've gotta call in a favor from someone I know I can trust. My brother here has a lady he needs taken to the safe house the boys up in Jersey City run. Some of them will still be awake at this hour. If not, here's some cash for a motel overnight. Get her in there first thing in the morning. Tell them things are even between us if they get this taken care of, alright?"

"Been a long time since I've been uptown," Eva says, stretching her arms and giving Mikhail a smile. "So am I following you, big guy?"

Mikhail gives a slow nod. "I appreciate it." He turns to me, a grateful look in those cold, killer's eyes of his. The eyes I know I share, deep down. This is the only person who knows me inside and out, but with Cherry at my side, I wonder if that might change.

"Leon, you should know of all people that I act swiftly and quietly. Once I'm off to handle this situation, it won't be long before it is done."

"I know," I say, glancing to Cherry and exchanging a look. "Tomorrow night, I'm guessing?"

Mikhail simply nods.

"Alright. I can work with that." The business silently concluded between us, there's suddenly a warmth in my eyes I haven't known in a long time, and I give my brother a smile. "It's been good to see you again, Mikhail."

The hitman's stony face shows the faintest smile, and before we know it, we're throwing our arms around each other, embracing fully for the first time in a very long while.

"Da svidaniya, Leon."

"Fsyevo harosheva, moy brat." The Russian language hasn't come from my mouth in a long time, and the words feel rusty yet familiar, like walking into an old childhood home after many years. It feels good.

We break our embrace, and I watch Mikhail, Alicia and Eva make their way across the bar and out the doors, into the cool night air.

I turn to Cherry, and something seems to be bothering her. I put my arm around her waist, and she hugs me back, laying her head against my chest briefly.

"So this is what it feels like," she says softly, and I look down at her.

"What do you mean?"

"Ordering someone's death. I mean, we've been in a firefight already tonight, but something about sending someone to carry it out deliberately feels so different. I just...I never thought I'd be in this position before, you know?"

I step in front of her, placing a hand on both of her shoulders gently and looking straight into those deep eyes of hers, searchingly. "And how do you feel about it now that you're here?"

The look she gives me back is brave. Cautious, but brave. "I don't know if this is going to work, Leon. It's a stretch. We're up against impossible odds, the other side has more resources than us, more people than us, and more information than us. *And* they have the law on their side. And at one flick of a wrist, they can have the public ready to take up arms against us." She pauses, but her eyes never break the gaze we share between us. "...but I agree. This needs to be done. I don't feel good about how it's going down, but Chandler's responsible for the deaths of a lot of innocent people, and he'll keep killing them as long as it lines his pockets." She takes a deep breath, as though re-centering herself. "No matter what happens, Leon, I'm standing by you."

Beaming at her, I hug her tight, breaking the seriousness of the moment with her yelp as I draw her into my embrace.

"I'm glad, because that's exactly what we're gonna do to establish an alibi."

"Wait, what?"

"You know as well as I do that when this goes down, all eyes are gonna be on us," I explain, crossing my arms. "So we need a really public display to prove that we're not involved. Mikhail won't leave a trace, so as long as it's well known that we're tied up somewhere else, nobody will be able to point a finger at us."

As she twirls a lock of hair thoughtfully over what I've just said, I lead Cherry over to where Genn has been finishing up the pool table on his own, and he gives us a nod as we approach. "'Sup, Prez?"

"Genn, we're having a bash tomorrow."

"A bash?"

"Yeah," I say, "there's been a real big fuckin' damper over the town since all this shit with the feds started going down. I want everyone to know that they can't keep us down. Show of solidarity that everyone can see — especially the feds."

Genn's started stroking his beard, and after a moment, he nods, and I can see the enthusiasm in him instantly. He's always been a sucker for parties like this.

"Alright, yeah. I like it. I've got a cousin who can get the word out around town, connected with just about half the damn city."

"Perfect," I say with a grin. "We'll hold it in the warehouse down at the end of Evergreen Street."

"Yeah, I remember that one," Genn laughs, remembering some old times fondly.

"Hear that, everyone?" I shout out across the bar, and the club turns to listen. "We're having our own little royal ball tomorrow night at the warehouse off Evergreen!"

A cheer goes up around the bar, and Cherry blinks in astonishment after some of the bikers group up as they start to file out for the night, discussing plans and what to bring.

"You've got a hell of a way of rallying people," she remarks.

"Comes in handy from time to time," I chuckle. "Come on, you're crashing at my place tonight."

She seems surprised as I lead her back to my bike, but I feel her arm wrap around my waist as I do, and I know she's happy with the arrangement. "Nobody's going to question an impromptu party in the middle of a war with the FBI, huh?"

"You must not have spent a lot of time around bikers, Cherry," I say in response, and she giggles lightly as we get pull out into the night.

In the back of my mind, I know there's another reason I want to set up this get-together. The thought has been in my mind since I claimed her on the hillside earlier tonight, ploughing her into my kutte with her ass slapping against me with each thrust.

I want everyone in the club to be really fucking clear about what Cherry is to me: *my old lady*.

*****

The way this town can pull something together last-minute never ceases to amaze me.

When news spread that the Union Club was hosting something this evening, it spread like wildfire. The town's been starving for something to raise their spirits, apparently. Before noon even rolled around, we were swamped with people calling club members to throw money into the thing and offer to cook or bring drinks. By the time people started showing up at the warehouse, you'd think it was a city-wide organized event.

I'm sitting at the end of a long table, laughing at one of Anya's jokes as we put down another beer. Cherry is on my lap, already blushing after a couple drinks, her arms around my neck.

There's music echoing throughout the whole warehouse, and Genn is up on the stage playing guitar with a handful of his buddies from work. He's had a garage band going for a few years, and he's been too shy to show it off to us, but his bandmates practically forced him to get up on stage with them for tonight.

Vasily and Roy are in the corner, taking on some of the locals at arm-wrestling. They threw together something of a tournament for the night, and now some of the factory workers from around town are trying their arms against them.

I practically ordered our bartender Rod to take the day off and enjoy himself, so I hired another local guy to run the show for him. He and I shot the breeze for a while before he snuck off to take part in what looked like a poker game among some of the other club members. Unfortunately for them, Rod has been around all of them long enough to know all their tells, and he's cleaning house, much to their chagrin.

Outside, I've heard that the mechanics from across town are being shown the club's bikes, and as news spreads, some of the club's gearheads slip out to take part. From what I've heard across the warehouse, Eva's already come close to getting into a brawl with someone over an engine modification.

"I can *not* believe I ever left this town," Cherry laughs as Anya slips off to chat with the young carpenter she's had her eye on all night. Cherry hugs my neck tight, planting a kiss on my cheek. "Leon, look at all this! This was less than a day's prep!"

"It's something else, yeah," I chuckle, giving her ass a squeeze and pulling her closer into me. She giggles, bringing her forehead to touch mine with heavily lidded eyes.

"I can't believe you, you know? It's like you can get this whole town moving, just by the force of your personality. But you don't use it for yourself, you know? You just kind of... inspire them."

The grin on my face spreads, and my hand runs up her back. "I'm not the only one who's inspired someone lately," I whisper in her ear in a husky tone, and Cherry bites her lip a moment before pressing her lips against mine.

I let her meld into me, tossing my beer aside as my hands grip her ass and we make out right there in view of everyone. It only makes my cock harder as I feel her up, and her hands slip inside my kutte while her tongue dives into my mouth.

"There's an empty office room in the back," I whisper into her ear, and she starts to grin and stand up when the warehouse front door swings open and Eva sprints in, waving her hands.

"Everyone! The feds are here!"

The next instant, half a dozen police officers flood through the door, one of whom grabs Eva's arms and presses her against the wall as he slips handcuffs on her wrists. A number of the cops shout out as they pour in: "County police! Everyone freeze, hands in the air!"

The crowd explodes.

Club members and townsfolk alike dive for windows, surge towards backdoors, or get run down by the county police. I realize that they're only grabbing the patches and anyone who's been seen with our club regularly.

Immediately, I grab a shocked Cherry's arm and bolt towards the back office I meant to fuck in a few moments ago.

Chaos takes over in a matter of moments, and my heart sinks as I hear Agent Doyle's voice just outside the entrance.

"FBI, FBI! Everyone remain calm, I have a warrant!"

Inside, things are anything but calm. The county sheriffs that have crashed the party waste no time in overturning tables, sending the home cooked food the town had brought in scattering across the floor, and the sound of broken glass tells me the drinks are following after in short order.

The club gets the worst of it. Vasily gets tackled by two of the cops, one of them sticking a knee in his neck while they handcuff him on the ground. It takes twice as many to keep Roy down. I don't see Anya or Genn, and I wonder whether they've already been hauled into the cars outside or if they made it out in time.

Cherry and I dart to the back office, and I make sure she's inside before glancing back at the front of the warehouse. Nobody seems to have noticed yet, but I can't count on that for long.

"Cherry," I breathe, slamming the door behind us and looking back at her, "there's a vent you can climb into here, just above that filing cabinet. Here, I'll help you up. Stay here until things cool off, they won't think to look for you."

"Wait," Cherry protests as I push her towards the cabinet, "what's going to happen to you?!"

"I don't know yet, Cherry. But if they've got us for the hit, then I'm sorry. You were right," I admit, a grim look on my face, but Cherry's face only shows concern for me.

"I don't see how, it isn't even that late yet, there's no way they could know about — "

Outside, I can hear footsteps getting closer, and the look on Cherry's face tells me she's heard it too. Without another word, I help her up, and she pries open the rusty vent shaft with little issue.

Whatever happens, Leon," she says as she clambers in, casting another look at me as I watch her slip inside, "I love you."

"I love you too, baby," "I say, my meaning absolute with every word. She closes the vent over her, and without another moment, I dart for the window on the other side of office. It would look suspicious if I was just standing there, but I know what's coming.

As if on cue, the door to the office smashes open just as my hands reach the window.

"That's far enough, Mr. Volkov," Agent Doyle says calmly, "you can keep your hands up against that window for us, thank you." I can practically hear the smile on his face.

"Sorry, did we forget your invitation?" I ask, keeping still as I three county sheriffs surround me and pull my arms behind me.

"Leon Volkov," Doyle proceeds, unfazed, "you are under arrest for obstruction of justice."

CHAPTER 19 - CHERRY

I hold my breath and watch in wide-eyed horror as Agent Doyle wrangles Leon's arms behind his back and clinks the handcuffs around his wrists. Part of me wants to kick the vent back open and launch myself at him, tackle that smarmy asshole to the ground and bloody his nose for daring to put his hands on Leon. But I know that anything I do now will only exacerbate the issue. I can't fight back that way. I'm not powerful enough to take anybody down with my strength (or lack thereof) and besides, we are outnumbered and outarmed.

The feds have legally-recognized and sanctioned weapons to use against us, and I'm just a skinny, trembling girl curled up in a dust-caked air vent.

So I have to bite my tongue and try not to breathe deeply while Doyle and his black-suited lackeys drag Leon away in cuffs, placing him under arrest. My heart is hammering loudly and I'm terrified that they might actually hear it. I cautiously wrap my arms around my chest as though to muffle the sound, my lungs growing tight and painful from holding in my breath for this long.

I wish Leon had actually escaped through the window. Maybe then he would have had a fighting chance. And he would have been able to evade arrest if not for the fact that he wasted time trying to conceal me and keep me safe. As the men leave the back office with Leon, I'm struck with mingled gratitude and overwhelming guilt, realizing just how much Leon might have just sacrificed for me. He didn't have to do that. He didn't *have* to take up precious seconds helping me into this air vent. God knows he's a fast enough runner — if only he had leaped out the window and took off into the sunset. But instead he put me first, willingly throwing himself under the bus just to give me a small chance at escape. And he did it without hesitation, without question, like it was an instinct rather than a conscious choice.

I don't think I've ever felt so protected and simultaneously so upset.

When I hear the last of the voices and scuffle fade away as everybody is either arrested and herded out the door or able to break free and run off, I take a deep breath at last. I want to punch myself in the face for letting Leon get in so much trouble over me.

Maybe if I had just minded my own business and stuck to my usual, stupid, pointless article content none of this would have happened. If I had just accepted my father's death as accidental rather than trying to build some big, overblown conspiracy around it, Leon would be okay. But no, I just couldn't keep myself out of trouble.

And now Leon is paying the price.

I sit here in the air vent beating myself up for what feels like at least an hour, too upset and afraid to move. I have no idea what to do, where to go from here. I've been following Leon's directions, tailing after him like a dopey, lovesick puppy, too enraptured to admit that I'm in way over my head. God, how could I have been so stupid?

My father would be so disappointed in me. We failed. And it's all my fault.

Without Leon to lead them, the Club will probably fall apart. And who knows if any of them even escaped from the party? Maybe they're all in handcuffs right now, being lugged off to jail, never to investigate anything else or save anyone else ever again.

Tears burn in my eyes and I angrily rub them away before finally stretching out my legs and carefully pushing the air vent open. Once the grate clatters to the ground, I extend one foot to cautiously get my balance on the filing cabinet beneath me. Then I slowly, carefully lower myself down through the square hole and clamber down the cabinet. I stand there in the empty room, looking around.

Then I tense up at the sound of footsteps.

Coming toward the door.

Oh, I'm an idiot! Of course the cops would still have someone stationed here just in case! And here I am, just standing here like a deer in the headlights, waiting to be cuffed and dragged away. But it hits me now that I don't really care. It's all over. There's no hope, anyway. Besides, I deserve to be arrested for the trouble I've caused.

So I just cross my arms over my chest and wait.

The door pushes slowly open, the rusting hinges whining. A tall, impossibly burly frame peeks around the door and walks into the room: Genn. I heave a sigh of relief.

"Oh, it's you," I murmur, exhaling deeply. Quickly, I add, "You escaped?"

Genn nods, scratching at the back of his head. "Yeah. I bolted when I heard the cops coming, hid in the musicians' van. None of them thought to check there, I guess. They just see motorcycles and think 'bad guy.' They didn't suspect any of us would be hiding in a van with an airbrush mural of a mermaid drinking vodka painted on the side of it."

"Hide in plain sight," comments a voice from behind him. I jump at the sound, but then Lukas shoves into the room, looking nearly apoplectic with rage. With his fists clenched at his sides and his teeth bared like a growling wolf, he swears, "Fucking rats. Just fucking stormed in here like they owned the place, but they're still too stupid to even get all of us."

"Who are you talking to? Someone in there?" pipes up another familiar voice. Vasily walks into the room, too, his eyebrows shooting up at the sight of me. "Cherry!" he gasps.

"How'd you manage not to get arrested? I saw that motherfucker Doyle and his stooges come into this room and grab Leon," Lukas asks, putting his hands on his hips.

I turn and point to the air vent. "Leon stashed me up in there. He — he took the time to hide me instead of just running away through the window like he should have," I explain, hanging my head guiltily. I expect Lukas to fly at me angrily and start cursing me. And I almost want him to.

Instead, Genn just says, "That sounds about right."

"Don't feel bad," Vasily says, shrugging. "He would never have let them take you. Just be glad he managed to find a way to save you without having to kill a cop or something."

"Yeah, you never had a choice in the matter," Lukas adds. "He would have literally shanked Agent Dickhead in the chest with a shard of glass or some shit, just to keep his old lady safe."

"So at least he's not going down for murdering a cop," Vasily says, genuinely relieved.

"What do we do now?" I ask, biting my lip, afraid of the answer. I want them to tell me there's a backup plan, that they're prepared for this kind of armageddon. I want them to give me the details to some over-the-top rescue mission they've been holding onto just for this kind of catastrophic turn of events.

But instead, they all just exchange world-weary looks.

"Good fucking question," Lukas comments bluntly.

"Well, the cops took him away, but surely we've got some guy on the inside who can help us out? A cop on the take who can break him out or at least relay us information?" I suggest, almost pleadingly. But Vasily shakes his head, giving me a pained expression.

"They're not taking him to the local precinct, Cherry," he tells me sadly. "Those weren't our usual everyday schmuck cops. Those were the feds and county sheriffs. They're taking him to the county jail."

"And we... we don't have anybody there?" I press weakly.

Lukas scoffs. "Hell no. Those guys are a little above our pay grade. It's hard enough to infiltrate the force here in Bayonne. But out there, things are tighter."

"The county guys aren't on our side," Vasily agrees. "They're in the pockets of the feds, and they're like the FBI's trained pitbulls when it comes to this stuff."

"And as you know, the feds are already more than okay with straight-up human trafficking and murder, so there's not really any chance of appealing to their moral conscience, either," Lukas snaps, gritting his teeth.

"This could be the end of the line," Genn concludes sorrowfully.

"But they don't know Leon is connected to the threat on Chandler's life," I remark, still trying desperately to hold this shitstorm together. "Doyle arrested him for obstruction — not murder or conspiracy or anything. Obstruction is, what, a misdemeanor?"

"They'll run it as a felony," Vasily says.

"And anyway that's just their excuse for dragging him in. Once they've got him in a cell, that'll give them plenty of time to find all kinds of other shit to pin on him," Lukas says.

"We — we can't give up this easily," I beg, shaking my head and taking a step forward. "It can't be over yet! Leon needs our help!"

"Cherry, we can't touch him now," Genn says gently.

I can't blame them for wanting to throw in the towel. After all, when I was sitting in that air vent just five minutes ago, I was thinking along the same lines. When things are this grim, it's definitely hard to see past it. But every time I think about how quickly Leon jumped to save me, throwing himself in the crosshairs just to give me a fighting chance — I realize that I won't be able to live with myself if I don't at least try to return the favor.

Besides, a life without Leon is not one I'm particularly interested in living anymore.

Not when his words are still ringing in my head: *I love you, too.*

"No," I protest, folding my arms across my chest defiantly. "I refuse to just lay down and let these feds ruin everything you all have worked so hard for. We've all come too far to just give up now."

"We'd probably only make it worse," Vasily comments, but I can tell he's starting to cave a little bit. There's a spark in his blue eyes indicating to me that he isn't ready to give up yet. I decide to stoke that tiny flame. If I'm really going to do this and take on the feds, I damn sure don't want to do it alone.

"Besides, we don't have anything on the feds," Genn says.

"They're dirty as fuck, but they're pros at looking squeaky clean," comments Lukas.

Suddenly I gasp, remembering something so small and seemingly insignificant that I did on a whim much earlier. Something I totally forgot in the rain of gunfire as we ran away from the docks the other night.

I took a picture with my phone at the scene of the crime.

"Hold on," I mumble, reaching into my jeans pocket to extract my cell phone. I scroll through the gallery of photos to find the blurry, grainy shot I took of Agent Doyle standing next to Chandler on the docks, overseeing the immigrants' grueling procession. I zoom in on Doyle's face. It's not the best quality photo, to be sure, but it definitely looks like him. Bingo.

"What are you doing?" Vasily asks, confused.

I hold up the phone for them to see the picture. "Look!"

All three of them lean in and squint at the phone screen. I wait expectantly for them to all realize just how valuable this evidence is. But instead they all just look defeated.

"Cherry, this is never gonna be enough," Genn tells me sympathetically.

"If a damning photograph was ever enough to put away a guy with this much immunity, God knows every one of those bastards would be behind bars by now," says Lukas.

"It's a good instinct," Vasily comments. "I'm glad you thought ahead to snap that picture in the moment, but I doubt it would ever be enough to do any real damage."

"You don't understand," I insist. "You can't underestimate the power of bad PR."

"Cherry, the FBI has enough PR points to commit mass murder and still come out spotless in the end," Vasily explains, but I can tell he wants so badly to believe.

"I *know* people. I'm a journalist, guys. Okay, I was never exactly Joseph Pulitzer, but that doesn't mean I don't have connections. I have the names and email addresses of so many editors — at least one of them will be interested in a story like this! Human trafficking! Murder conspiracies! Dirty feds! Everybody loves a good underdog story," I ramble, feeling my face grow flushed with enthusiasm.

Vasily looks like he might actually join my crusade. He turns to Genn and Lukas, who look much more dubious, regarding both of us with suspicious expressions.

"It might be worth a shot," he begins hesitantly.

"It might do more harm than good," Genn says. "And if they find out the leak came from you, Cherry, you'll be putting yourself directly in danger."

"I made my decision the second I met Leon, whether I knew it then or not," I assure him confidently. And deep down, I know it to be true. "If loving him means that I have to spend the rest of my life on the edge, that's what I'll do. He put his life on the line for me, and it's only right I do the same for him."

Lukas grins, to my complete surprise. "Damn, Cherry. You're a tougher kid than I thought. I'm really starting to dig having you around."

"Okay, we can all do a group hug later," Vasily cuts in, his face serious.

"Who are you gonna send the photo to?" Genn asks.

I'm already scrolling through my contacts, looking for one name in particular. When I first moved to New York City, I had a brief internship at what I call "a real newspaper." It paid a pittance barely enough to get me a 300-

square-foot hole in the wall on Staten Island, but it gave me insight into what it's like publishing articles that really change the world. I only filed papers and fetched coffees and snacks for the editorial staff, but my cutesy name and upbeat personality helped me stand out among the other tight-lipped, buttoned-up interns. The head editor-in-chief always had a soft spot for me, giving me the kind of glowing recommendation letters that helped me land my cushy, albeit inconsequential, jobs writing puff pieces.

I find her name in my contact list and my thumb hovers over it, hesitating. I have not spoken to her in months. She may not even remember me anymore — she's a high-powered editor who talks to a hundred people a day. It's easy to get lost in a crowd that big.

But I have to try, for Leon's sake. Because I love him.

So I send her a long email with the photo of Doyle and Chandler, detailing the situation and their respective roles. The three club guys watch silently as I type out the email and click send. Then I look up at them and say, "It's done."

"Who'd you send it to?" Vasily asks, concerned.

"An old editor friend," I explain simply. I don't tell them that she was only my boss for six months and I haven't spoken to her in a long time. They don't need to know that right now.

"And you think she'll side with us?" Genn pipes up.

I nod firmly. "I know she will." Ellen Hardy was always suspicious of all law enforcement, and her paper often focused on issues of police corruption and other similar topics. She'll jump at the opportunity to run a story like this.

"So what now? How long do we wait for her response?" Lukas demands impatiently.

Just then, my phone lights up. Ellen's email back comes instantaneously, containing a brief thank you and a phone number next to the word 'FBI' in bold.

She's given me a direct line to the FBI. At the bottom of the email, there's a line that reads: *PS - You make the call. We'll light up the print. Good to have you back.*

I press the number and hold the phone to my ear, my heart pounding as it starts to ring.

"Who are you calling?" Vasily asks, his blue eyes wide and round.

"The FBI," I answer flatly.

CHAPTER 20 - LEON

"How many times have we gotta go through this song and dance, Agent Boyle? You know for a fact I'm the most upstanding citizen in this whole damn city." It gets to him when I mess up his name, even though he tries not to show it.

"We're not in the city of Bayonne's jurisdiction, Mr. Volkov," Agent Doyle says, pacing around the interrogation table once again. This time, though, I can see a certain excitement in his eyes, and I have to admit that it's not entirely unfounded. He has a hell of an upper hand here.

"You're in the county lockup, and well within my jurisdiction now." He takes a few steps forward, crossing his arms and sneering at me. "But you really should be more careful at those wild parties of yours — it looks like you got into one too many fistfights with your criminal associates."

He's talking about my swollen lip, black eye, and the trickle of blood running from a cut in my forehead. Not to mention all the bruises I can feel forming on my chest from the pummeling I've taken since getting in here. The moment I was behind a closed door, Doyle turned his pigs loose on me. The young bucks at the county sheriff's office were eager to get their hands on a man like me. Doyle "turned a blind eye" to me for a good half hour before returning to start the official interrogation.

But I wasn't going to let him have the satisfaction of seeing me in pain, so I spat what blood I had in my mouth onto the floor and kept that same old grin on. After all, I still have all my teeth. It's driving him nuts, too.

"First of all, we have your men roaring up to a murder investigation, potentially endangering the crime scene and any evidence that may have been essential to the investigation, besides harassing officers of the law."

"Trying to pin something some friends of mine did of their own accord on me after letting me go last time? That's just shoddy detective work."

Doyle's fist clenches, but as long as the little red light is on the camera that's pointed at me, I know I can goad him as much as I like, if he wants to keep his career. There's a lot more buttons I know I could push on Doyle, but I also know that the camera's gonna get shut off sooner or later, and this is a man who doesn't bat an eye at burying immigrants in unmarked graves.

"You proceeded to put together a rally orchestrated by the Union Club in an attempt to align Bayonne citizens against law enforcement, are you aware that some would call that 'rabble rousing,' Mr. Volkov?"

I laugh at that, though it hurts a few ribs to do so.

"I think the good people of Bayonne would *love* to hear you call them rabble, *pizdoon.*"

"What was that, Mr. Volkov?"

"That was Russian, Agent McCarthy. You might do well to learn a little bit about the heritage of a town before you go harassing its workers. Or maybe that's not really why you're here?"

Doyle keeps his eyes even on mine for a while, studying my face before smiling. "I'm here to enforce the law, Mr. Volkov, nothing more. While we're on the topic of your Russian heritage, though, maybe you can speak for some of your other *gang* members' actions, hm?"

I snort in derision at the word *gang*. It got under my skin once, but not now. This is all an act. Doyle is just trying to wave the fact over my head that he's got half the club locked up and *maybe* get enough of a rise out of me to incriminate one of them. I know all his tricks.

"Ms. Eva Zolnerowich, for starters. You know, the mechanics we interviewed after the arrests admitted that she was soliciting illegal vehicle modifications to them? How long has the Union Club been in the business of peddling street wares, Mr. Volkov?"

He wants me to say that I can't account for the actions of my cohorts, but that would just incriminate Eva, and I'm not gonna throw my VP under the bus like that.

"I'm failing to see what your accusations have to do with 'obstruction of justice,' Agent Toyle."

My name-calling seems to push Doyle over the edge, and he slams his fist onto the table, leaning in close to me. "Do you want me to tack on 'badgering an officer' to the laundry list I'm about to throw you away for, you little shit?"

I just smile at him in response, and I think I can see a little vein pulsing in his forehead as he steps back.

"Mr. Gennedy Alkaev, another of your officers, wasn't apprehended at the scene. You ought to know that was because he's been working with us since your first arrest, Mr. Volkov. He tipped us off about your little rally and let us show up in time to break things up before it got violent. How does it feel that your supposedly loyal little personality cult is willing to sell you out?"

I say nothing in response. I know that's a lie. It has to be. Genn's more than a gentle soul with a ton of muscle padding it — he's a close friend. Cherry is a good judge of character, and she seems to get along with him fine, to boot. That on top of his years of friendship to me are more than enough proof that Doyle's lying through his teeth.

When I keep quiet for a few seconds more, Doyle lets out a long breath and moves over to the camera, shutting it off.

"Alright then, let's talk," he says, walking over to sit on the table beside me, peering down at me through his glasses. I have a feeling he gets off on looking down at people like that.

"Tell me, Mr. Volkov, how much did you and that little cunt you've been dragging around with you see down at the docks the other night?" he asks in a still, quiet voice. My eyes narrow at him, and I lean forward in my chair, looking at him as though daring him to keep going. "Any of the 'cargo' look familiar? Did you recognize some of those corpses' relatives in those containers? Mothers, children?"

My jaw is tight, and I feel my hands flexing into fists. There it is: Doyle's confession. He's got me locked away, and this whole interrogation is just a farce to cover up whatever trumped-up charge he'll pin on me.

"Did your parents get here by similar means, Mr. Volkov? Is that why you're so insistent on disrupting my business with

Marty Chandler? Maybe you had a sister who met a similar fate on a voyage over here, is she buried out back behind your bar?"

My teeth are grinding together, and it's taking everything in me not to break his nose. It's within reach. I'm not restrained, and I want nothing more than to get my hands on him. But I don't let him have that. I won't give him something to pin on me. And I can see how furious my patience is making him as his eye twitches just a hair.

"My business with Marty Chandler is good, but it isn't even my biggest paycheck, you know? Just a side gig. Maybe it'll pay for a vacation to TJ next year, and I'll get to fuck some of the relatives of the people I've shipped over, all while you're rotting in jail for the next few years. If you make it that long, mind you — I'm sure there was someone underage at that party, and you know how well statutory rapists fare in prison."

My face is stony as I stare him down, and it finally breaks him. He brings his fist around and right into jaw, and I feel blood in my mouth as he leans forward, grabbing hold of the scruff of my collar.

"Maybe while you're gone, I'll have that cunt of yours shipped down to Mexico in return for being so nosy. I can't believe you'd go through all this shit for her. All because her old man stuck his nose into our business and had to be taken care of?"

With one hand, I seize Agent Charles Doyle by the arm and hurl him over the table, slamming him down and leaping up on top of him.

One of my fists connects with his nose before he knees me sharply in the stomach, shoving me off onto the floor, but before he can fumble for his gun, I leap up and turn the table over, knocking him back and sending him into the wall with a thud as I hop over the table.

We grapple as I reach him, his hands around my neck and mine on his collar, slamming him into the wall behind him as his weak arms try to squeeze the breath out of me. His glasses have fallen off, and I can see the nothing but hatred in his beady eyes. One of his hands lets go of my neck to go for his gun, and once again, I hurl him around, sending him toppling to the ground into the overturned table.

Before he can get his bearings, though, this time I dive on top of him, and my hand goes straight for his gun at the same time his does.

I'm faster.

In the span of a breath, I snatch Doyle's gun from his side and point it at his head as I slip the safety off and cock it.

CHAPTER 21 - CHERRY

Despite how dire this situation is, I can't help but stifle a giggle at how ridiculous Genn looks hunched over in the passenger seat of my Ford Focus. The tiny car suits me just fine — and it's appropriately sized for most normal people, too. But Genn is roughly the size of a grizzly bear, and he has to fold his arms inward and bow his head slightly just to fit, even after scooting the seat back as far as it can go. He's rolled down the window, gazing out at the passing trees and highway signs as we blow down the road toward the county lockup.

I don't exactly know what to expect when we get there. After talking to Ellen Hardy a little more, she advised me to take on this story myself. She called me last night while I was meeting up with Genn, Vasily, Lukas, and a couple other Club members at the Glass.

To my infinite surprise, she informed me that she's been charting my progress, following my career ever since my internship with her paper ended. At first, I was embarrassed to find this out — after all, I haven't exactly been taking on the hard-hitting, breaking news articles she printed all the time. The idea of Ellen Hardy, the powerful and influential mentor I idolized for months, reading my frilly fashion pieces was enough to make me want to crawl into a hole and never come back out.

She revealed to me that she's actually been hoping I would come back and apply for a position on her team for awhile now, and that despite the frivolous nature of my work, my strong voice manages to shine through.

"I know you're not living up to your full potential," she told me, "but I wanted you to know that your talent has not gone unnoticed. I don't know what the hell you're doing in Jersey, or how you've sniffed out a scoop as big as this one, but I do know that your passion and your eye for detail qualify you as the best journalist to follow it. I will give you any information, any resource I can possibly provide, if you promise to write this article for me. This will change everything, Cherry. People need to know what's going on down there in New Jersey. And when you're done… just know there will always be an open slot for you back here in the Big Apple."

I had just sat there in silent disbelief for a minute, letting all of this sink in. Here, I had assumed Ellen would sic one of her star journalists on the story, fly them down here to badger the everloving shit out of the cops until they gave up enough information for a sellable story.

Instead, she asked me to do it. She wanted me to write it.

It's a dream come true — wrapped up in the trappings of my worst nightmare.

Because now not only do I have to find a way to free Leon and put a stop to the illicit affairs going down in Bayonne, I also have to write a kick-ass, no-holds-barred story about the whole shebang. But I couldn't say no.

"Cherry? Are you there? What do you say?" Ellen had pressed.

Quickly I replied, "Yes. Yes, absolutely I will write it."

And now here I am, driving down the highway dressed in my dark jeans, black blouse, black blazer, and — for once — comfortable shoes bought just this morning. If I'm gonna bust into the county jail guns a-blazin' with Genn by my side to rescue my biker boyfriend, I damn well better wear my running shoes.

"Thanks for coming with me," I blurt out suddenly. Genn looks over at me with compassionate eyes. He reaches across the console to pat my arm.

"Of course. You're the brains, I'm the brawn. We make a good team," he replies with an easygoing smile. Truth be told, I'm relieved he's the one coming with me. I really like everyone in the Club, but Genn is such a teddy bear, he's fast become my favorite.

Well, except for Leon.

And the two of us are both dogged and determined to get Leon out of jail and clear his name. Genn's his best friend, and I'm… his girlfriend. His Old Lady, I inwardly correct myself, and I feel a bit giddy at the distinction. Because you can't go through what we've gone through together without skipping a few steps in the relationship timeline.

So Genn and I are on the way to catch Leon and tell him everything we've found out, all the incriminating evidence we have on Doyle and Chandler, tell him we can take these bastards down without having to shed any more blood. And the feds are on their way to arrest Doyle, having finally caught on to the fact that he's a dirty cop. But they don't know who I am. Their information came from a journalist with a major paper — me. I knew they wouldn't take the information seriously if it came from someone already associated with Leon Volkov and the Club so I didn't mention it.

I just hope we get there before it's too late.

As far as Leon knows, things are still dire. The county cops are probably goading him to hell, trying as hard as they can to force him into a corner. And when you corner a guy like Leon, he isn't going to take it without a fight. Genn and I are going there to stop that from happening.

"Here, take a right on this exit," Genn says suddenly. I pull the car onto the ramp and down a hill, then we drive for a few miles under Genn's instructions until finally the building comes into view. My heart sinks at the sight of the ten-foot-tall chain link fence blocking our entrance.

"Oh no," I murmur, "what are we gonna do?"

"Listen," Genn whispers, holding up one finger. We hear the approaching squeal of tires and manage to pull the Focus off the road into a clearing behind a patch of trees just before a cavalcade of black sedans come thundering up to the gate.

"The feds," I whisper, feeling nauseous. They've beaten us here. If they see me or Genn, they'll immediately suspect something's off. All they know is that Leon is innocent and that Doyle is not. Genn and I are still just trespassing citizens, and it doesn't help that we're both associated with the Club. These guys won't recognize us on sight, I'm sure, but if they arrest us, our identities will inevitably come up. Even if the feds can't pin this particular crime on us, they'll never really be on our side — they'll lock us up without a second thought.

"Look, the gate's opening. What if we just...?" Genn trails off, raising an eyebrow questioningly. I catch his drift. We both shrug and jump out of the car, bolting after the sedans through the fence just before it closes again, my heart racing.

God, I hope they don't arrest us, too!

"Genn, hide," I hiss, waving my hand to shoo him off. He nods and wordlessly darts off the path into the shade of some trees and underbrush while I walk confidently up the driveway, even though I'm not sure if the plan I'm formulating on the way there is going to blow up in my face. Part of me wants to just tell them why I'm here, but I can't risk muddying up their case against Doyle.

Still, I've got to try something. *Fake it till you make it*, I urge myself as I strut up through the rows of black sedans. The feds are pouring out now, holding up their hands to stop me, shouting at me to get back and stay back.

I simply hold my hands up in surrender and announce, "I'm a journalist! The people have a right to know about what Leon Volkov has done! I'm here to collect the truth and by God I am going to get it even if I have to spend the night in a cell to do so!"

"Ma'am, the press is not allowed beyond that gate!" bellows one of the agents, his shiny aviator sunglasses reflecting my own passionate face as he storms up to me.

"This is public property! I am a tax-paying citizen who just wants to share information with other upstanding citizens about what's going on here today!" Deciding it can't hurt to lay it on thick, I continue, "Leon Volkov is a career criminal with no soul and I am here to make sure the world knows that our police are bringing him to justice!"

I can see some of the feds relaxing a bit, believing I'm just some ignorant media peon. At least they're less likely to arrest me now, even if they're still not willing to let me inside the building.

"Miss, I apologize, but you can't go in there with us, as much as we'd like to let you in," says another agent, removing his sunglasses to wink at me.

I bat my eyelashes and twirl a loose lock of hair around my finger, trying my best to look demure and innocuous. "It's just that… I have a real passion for seeing bad guys nailed to the wall for their crimes and, well, it would really make my year to catch a scoop like this one."

I can tell a couple of the feds want to let me in, but the first guy who approached me is still standing his ground, his mouth set in a hard line. He clearly doesn't want a reporter finding out that one of the FBI's own is really the big baddie behind the crime. I'm starting to see the flaws in my last-minute plan now.

Not looking away from me for a second, he orders, "All of you inside. I'll deal with this."

Reluctantly, the other agents file into the building and fear floods my veins as I'm left all alone with the big bad fed. He takes my arm and starts pulling me away, back toward the gate. "You've got to leave immediately, ma'am. I don't know how you got in here or why you thought you have any right to just show up like this, but — "

Just then, Genn leaps out of the bushes and cocks a gun I didn't know he had, pointing it straight at Mr. Special Agent beside me. "Let go of the bitch!" he shouts, and I instantly realize that Genn is trying to create a distraction.

A very, very dangerous one.

He's aiming a gun at a federal agent! Within two seconds, the fed releases me and pulls out his own gun to point it at Genn. "Drop the weapon!" commands the agent.

Before I can think twice, I'm bolting toward the county lockup.

"If you make one move toward her I will fire!" Genn is shouting behind me, and I know he's got the agent stuck there.

My heart is pounding in my ears as I throw open the doors to the building and yell, "Rogue agent is about to shoot a civilian out there!"

A stampede of agents go thundering toward the door and I use the momentary mayhem to slip past the security stop and bolt down the hallway to what I hope to be the interrogation room. I only have a minute or so before anyone catches on and realizes what I'm doing back here, so I pick the very first door and swing it open.

I gasp and cover my mouth at the sight of Leon standing up in the middle of the room, his back facing me. The wooden table and rickety chairs have been flipped over and kicked aside and Leon is pointing a gun at the officer in the corner…

It's Doyle!

Leon must have somehow grappled the gun away from the bastard during a scuffle. I can't let Leon make the mistake of murdering a federal agent just when everything is finally about to be resolved.

"Stop!" I cry out, my voice shaking.

I hear voices and heavy footsteps pounding up the hallway toward this room, one of them possibly belonging to Genn. I wonder if he managed to convince the feds he's on their side, after all. God, we should have just told them who we were!

Leon doesn't look back at me, but he struggles to keep his voice even when he replies softly, "Cherry, you have to go. I won't let you see this."

"I'm not going anywhere!" I shout. "Don't shoot him!"

"This bastard deserves everything he gets! He killed your dad, Cherry!" Leon yells, flicking the trigger.

Doyle flinches, but he says, "Listen to your girlfriend, Volkov. It's all over. You're going away for a very, very long time."

"No, Charlie. You are," says a deep voice behind me. The agent who grabbed me earlier pushes me aside, walking into the room with his own gun raised — at Leon. "Drop the gun, Volkov. You're free to go."

"Is this some kind of trick?" Leon demands, not daring to look away from Doyle.

"No, Leon! They're here to arrest Doyle. I talked to the FBI and told them everything. I gave them evidence. I — I came here to tell you so you wouldn't do anything stupid," I ramble quickly, tears pulsing down my cheeks. I can't stand to see Leon like this, pushed to the edge of desperation, thinking he would have to kill Doyle himself to get justice for all those poor people.

"Lower the weapon, son," says the agent.

"Don't let him shoot me!" Doyle wails.

"Shut your mouth," the agent barks. Doyle goes pale, finally realizing he's actually going down for good. This isn't a game.

Reluctantly, Leon bends down and sets the gun on the floor.

"Good man," the agent says, walking past him to jerk Doyle up by the collar. Two more agents file into the room to wrest Doyle's hands behind his back and cuff him.

Leon finally turns around and looks at me, his green eyes bright even under the dim lighting of a single, flickering lightbulb above us. He's got a black eye, as well as bruises and lacerations up and down his arm and neck. They really beat the hell out of him here.

"Cherry," he murmurs, saying my name like a prayer.

I rush into his arms and press my face into his chest, my tears staining his shirt. He embraces me and kisses the top of my head, stroking my hair. "I'm so sorry we took so long," I whimper, clinging to him.

"No, no, I'm sorry you had to see me that way."

"Well, if you aren't a sight for sore eyes," Genn says jovially, standing in the doorway.

"Genn! What the hell did you say to them to get out of that mess I caused?" I ask incredulously, utterly relieved to see him alive and in one piece. After all, I did inadvertently sic a pack of armed federal agents on him out there.

He shrugs. "I told them the truth. Turns out it really does set you free. Oh, and the gun wasn't loaded."

The three of us walk out of the building, Genn running ahead to catch up with the feds and talk to them. Battered and broken as he is, Leon smiles as the sun hits his face. He wraps an arm around me and spins me to face him. Then he leans down and kisses me hard on the lips, his fingers tangling in my hair. We stand this way for awhile, wrapped up in each other, all too relieved and elated to be together once again — alive and free at last.

CHAPTER 22 - LEON

With Doyle in jail, the police are reeling from lack of support up top. The rest of the club that was arrested gets released along with me, given that Doyle's entire operations in Bayonne were invalidated in light of his corruption. Besides, pressing charges now for the stuff they might actually have on the club would only bring more heat down on them. They want to take care of this as quietly as possible.

I get news from Mikhail that Marty Chandler died silently around the same time

Doyle was smugly arresting me in the warehouse office. By all rights, it looked like a car accident, and neither Doyle nor the county sheriffs knew anything about it as it pertained to us. With that information, we don't waste any time in busting up all the illicit rings Doyle spent so long raking in profits from.

We start where it all began, at the dockyards in Bayonne. While the police who've been on the take for years watching their superior officers get away with murder get to finally arrest all the dock bosses who've been taking part in the human trafficking ring, the club and I team up with some medical personnel to free the immigrants locked up in the freighter.

Me, Cherry, and the rest of the club personally help unload them all as the medical staff on hand start tending to their injuries—the healthiest of them are dehydrated, but catching this when we did has saved a lot of lives, one of the paramedics informs us.

A few hours into the rescue, Cherry makes her way over to me as Genn and I help lift an older man onto a gurney with one of the paramedics.

"One of the nurses who speaks Spanish was able to talk to one of the victims," she explains as we finish and turn to her. "Between the two of us, we were able to interpret that Doyle's had a hand in facilitating these operations all up and down the seaboard. There's a ton of operations like this one taking place."

"Shit," Genn says, "so what, there's a string of Agent Doyles keeping these rings up and running?"

"On the contrary," Cherry says, and I see a spark of investigative fire in her eyes that makes me want to kiss her, "with Doyle's arrest, any other corrupt federal support is going to go into hiding, fast. This could be the one moment in a long time all those trafficking rings are vulnerable to being busted, hard."

A smile crosses my face, and I fold my arms, looking out over the Bayonne public servants working together with the club to make a real difference in these people's lives. I exchange glances with Genn, whose expression tells me he's thinking the same thing I am.

"If that's the case," I say to Cherry, "then there's no time to lose, is there?"

"Think you're right, Prez," Genn answers with a grin. "I'll go look for Eva and get the club riled up. Think it might be time for us to expand out?"

"We're not the only town that's been hurting because of Doyle's trafficking, and without the club, this would've been a lot worse. I think it's time."

Cherry watches him go with a satisfied look in her eye at the prospect of the club taking action again, but there's something in that gorgeous face of hers that's bothering her.

"What's the matter, something up?"

"Hm? Oh, no," she gives her head a shake. "I mean...if you and the Union are headed out to ride, that means 'goodbye' again, doesn't it?"

I laugh out loud, throwing my arm around her and yanking her into my side to her surprise before pressing a deep kiss into her. She yelps, but then her body relaxes and gives a soft moan at my kiss.

"Are you kidding?" I finally whisper when we break apart, but I keep her in my grip. "You've done more investigative work for us than anyone has been able to in all the years we've been protecting this town. We'll *need* you to help us bust up these fuckers. And besides," I add with a wink, "I think it's about time you really saw the States from the back of a motorcycle anyway, and I don't have any intention of letting you leave my side. And hey, should make one hell of a story: reporter travels up and down the coast, busting human trafficking rings and rallying the underdogs."

Her mouth starts to spread into a smile as I speak, and she bites her lip to try and hold it back, but by the end of it, she just puts her hands on my face and pulls herself up into another deep kiss while Genn explains the situation to the rest of the club not far from us.

*****

We ride the very next day.

The wind whips across my face, my knuckles are bitten by the dust of the road, and my kutte flaps around me as I lead our pack of bikes down the interstate, heading south. Men and women I can trust with my life are behind me, the open road is ahead of me, and if that weren't enough, the most brilliant and gorgeous woman I've ever met has her arms wrapped around my waist, her heart beating furiously at the first taste of real freedom out here.

We carve a path from city to city, county to county, state to state, starting south in Delaware and Maryland before whipping around north across New York and onward to Connecticut. With each stop, Cherry gets more shrewd at gathering information for the club to use, identifying crooked cops, bought judges, and fat-cat bosses after each lead.

The immigrants rescued from Bayonne didn't know much, but a laptop Mikhail confiscated from Marty Chandler's house provided more than a few leads for us to go on. The nearest connection the slimeball had was just a few towns over, and that proved to be only the beginning of a long string of rings. Every local crime lord had tangential connections nearby just like Marty, and once Cherry was able to establish a pattern to fill in the blanks left by Mikhail's evidence, the rest was just a matter of the Union Club doing what it does best.

The first bust goes down just a few towns south of Bayonne. After Cherry's secured a solid lead to a warehouse down by the docks, our bikes roar out to the site on a night a shipment's supposed to be made, according to a dock worker with a conscience. The moment our headlights shine on the armed men bringing in living cargo around midnight, shots start going off.

As it turns out, most of the goons hired to ship the immigrants in aren't paid well enough to stick around once we've turned up the heat. Our club knows how to handle itself in a firefight, and it isn't long before most of the creeps go running for the hills, leaving us to take the law into our own hands with the dock owners who make it all happen. But not before we put down a few of their men, and they give us a few injuries in return. Anya's going to have her work cut out for her over the next few weeks.

The situation is dealt with, and just as expected, when we call the hospital in to tend to the immigrants, there's no voice up top telling them to hold back; the feds are in hiding, and we've struck while the iron is hot.

One of the locals tips us off about a brothel a few towns further south, and we're off again. It's an even simpler job—our bikes come roaring off the interstate, surround the house where the sex slavery ring is operating, and before the pimps know what's pulled up on their front porch, we're kicking down the doors and taking over the place.

It doesn't take long for us to get a reputation. After a few more towns, bosses and crime lords alike start getting nervous at the news of our kutte being spotted on the roads nearby. The sounds of our engines tearing into a dock or a warehouse district sends the slavers running, and the ones that put up a tough fight quickly find themselves outmatched.

Part of that is because as news of our work starts to spread, other bikers start paying attention. A few trustworthy guns for hire start snowballing into our ragtag pack of ex-dock workers, and as we fan out north, we've nearly doubled our numbers.

The whole ride takes over a month. By the end of it, we have a reputation as one of the most feared clubs on the eastern seaboard, but the only ones cowering are the human traffickers. Just like the crooked opportunists took advantage of the FBI's presence in town, word of our vigilantism emboldens the workers from town to town, and before long, we start hearing about miners and factory laborers and dock workers organizing themselves and pushing out internal corruption on their own, before we even hit the town.

But after a long and hard streak across New England, the time comes for us to head back to where it all got started—back to Bayonne, where the townspeople greet our ride into the city with a celebration.

Eva heads off to lead one of the branches of the Union Club that's cropped up in upstate

New York, and I give her all the best as she does. Genn sticks by my side, despite having the chance to do the same, but he just laughs the offer off and says his place is right here in Bayonne. Since Eva will take up the rank of President at her own branch, I give Genn her old spot as Vice-Prez, and Vasily takes his place as my Sergeant. Anya will have an officer's rank with her name on it too, if she can keep her hands off Officer Samuels long enough. Well, it isn't 'officer' anymore since he quit the force to join the Club, but the boys seem to like it as a nickname for him.

But I'm most impressed of all with Cherry. She's a natural at this, to the point that she loses herself talking about leads and new connections even during our downtime. Now that we're back in Bayonne, though, I'm forcing all of us to take a little downtime in our own ways.

And my downtime with Cherry is what I'm looking forward to more than anything.

CHAPTER 23 - CHERRY

He pushes me through the door to his room with his ravenous kisses, his hungry, powerful arms gripping me all over my body as he explores me with utter abandon. All of our restraint has long been gone, but now that the storm is past us, it feels all the more thrilling.

Even as we stumble through his room to the bed, his mouth is at my neck, and I'm rolling my head back with a breathy gasp as his hand works itself down my pants, expertly finding my slit and starting to rub it voraciously. Behind me, his other hand squeezes my ass. He wants me so badly, and I couldn't stand not to have him inside me for another minute.

He tears my clothes off urgently. His need for me is just as bad as mine for him, even if it is a little more disorganized, more animalistic. I can hear it in his grunts, his breaths, and of course, I can feel it in the hardness between his legs.

The steady, untamed hum of a motorcycle under me has become comfortable over the past few weeks. I thought the thrill of it would wear off after a while, but it's become only more exciting over time, the vibration only more arousing, especially with Leon in front of me.

Leon. God, I never saw any of this coming, I realize. A few weeks ago, I was just another journalist doing puff pieces, and then we storm into each other's lives. I feel a laughing smile sneak up across my face as I think about the two of us as a pair of investigative vigilantes, and Leon breaks away from my face after laying me down on the bed and grins back at me.

"What's that for?"

"I was just thinking how weird it is, how this all worked out," I say, reaching up and letting my hand brush across his rough stubble. "You were just some vagrant I thought was beating up shopkeepers when I came back to town."

"You're not completely wrong," he answers, and I give him a playful push while we laughs, but it only teases him on, and in another moment, his hands are on my breasts, savoring their feel as he grinds his hips up into me. I close my eyes and let myself revel in the sensation, in the feeling of this fiery rebel claiming me and every part of my body. Then I gasp as he takes a handful of my hair, holding me with a strong grip as he leans in to whisper into my ear.

"We did a hell of a lot before you got here," he growls in a low tone, "but fuck, Cherry. Everything I really want to remember happened after you got back into my life."

Now my hips are pushing back up against the stiff bulge in his pants, and my breaths are coming hot and heavy, I realize. Even without my conscious willing, my body wants him. I need him, and now.

My bra is already halfway across the room as he works off my pants. He's not gentle, and

I love it. Living this life on the road, rough and dirty, tracking down criminals and putting our lives on the line for the greater good every day, it's awakened something in me I never knew I had. I feel more alive coming home from a day tracking down traffickers and getting my clothes ripped off roughly by Leon than I ever did in a cozy apartment in New York.

He works his own pants off next, one hand holding my hair while the other pushes up the small of my back, and he isn't wasting any time in pressing his bare cock up against me. I look down and see his dark crown, bulging in need before me as he presses it against the surface of my cunt, and I gasp.

We've had so little privacy over the past few weeks, sharing motel rooms with the club and riding from sunrise to sunset. How many times have I seen him, gun out and blazing with a fierce glint to his eye, knowing he's fighting for people who can't fight for themselves? How often have I seen him putting his life on the line to bring justice to people who've bought their way out of the law's justice their whole lives?

Each and every time made my desire for him grow all the stronger, fanning my lust into something beyond my control. I'd grip him as we rode the day after, letting my hands trail to his cock and rub up against him, and all that tension felt so fucking good to finally *let go*.

I let out a scream of all that release when his cock impales me.

Immediately, his hips are like a piston in my slick insides. My cunt has been ready for him all afternoon, knowing we'd be back in town and in private again. Finally.

His cock feels bigger than ever, swollen with desire for me, precum mixing with my honey as he bucks into me, and I thrust my hips up in rhythm with him.

He reaches up and grips the backboard of the bed, pounding up into me more and more fiercely, and my hands slide up to his rock-hard abs, feeling every muscle and ripple in his hardened body.

This man is a killer. You've seen him kill in front of your very eyes, and he used to do it for money. What the hell are you doing, Cherry?

I'm doing something better for myself than I've ever done before, I realize as I clench my cunt tightly around his shaft, stars in my eyes as he bucks wildly into me.

"I'm all yours, Leon," I moan, "fuck, I've wanted you to ride me like this from the moment I saw you!"

He doesn't respond with words, animalistically pounding into me all the more fiercely, and he looks down at me with those piercing eyes of his. Through all the fire, all the passion, I can see something more behind that gaze.

"I love you, Cherry," he says at last, slowing his pumping just enough to bend down and kiss me deeply, and my hand reaches up to meet his face and pull it into me.

As he does, I arch my back up into him, and while we kiss, I feel my orgasm boil up within me, and I moan loudly into his kiss, my cunt tightening and my honey flooding his shaft. I never want the kiss to break. I want to stay here, with him inside me, and I want him to fill me up entirely.

The harsh bucking he responds to my tightness with tells me he can pick up on my desire, like a musk in the air. I'm his. He's mine. And I never want that to change.

"I love you, Leon," I gasp, each word punctuated by a breath as he rams into me, the tip of his dark, purple crown striking the inner depths of my cunt, harder and fiercer than ever before. As his balls slap against me, they start to tighten, and his cock swells up within me even more.

"Fuck," he groans, and as I open my eyes to look at him, he isn't closing his eyes to revel in his impending orgasm — he's looking straight into my eyes.

As I look into the face of that untamed man from my past, I feel my own cunt starting to tighten again, and my mouth hangs open involuntarily as everything within me starts to come to a great, disjointed rise.

His hot, dominant seed shoots up into me, and I feel a body-wracking orgasm shake every nerve in my body, my eyes rolling up into my head as all of my senses are overwhelmed under him. He lets out a throaty groan, and I can tell that every part of him is just as ecstatic as he pours himself into me, and I can feel all my insides getting filled up by him as he puts his hands on my hips, pulling me further up onto his spear as we come together.

As the last of his seed spills into me, he stays hard, gently rocking back and forth as we just kind of look into each other's eyes, stillness descending like a spell all around the simple room. All we can focus on is each other, and it's wholly and utterly satisfying.

"You know," I whisper to him after who knows how long, his cock pulsing within me softly, "I was wrong about you, Leon."

"How's that?" he asks with a small, cocky smile.

"For the longest time, I thought you were just a bandit under another name."

"You were right," he says, pressing into me a little further, still hard as a rock, and I gasp involuntarily. "Only difference is, I do it for a better cause."

A long pause passes between us as I just smile up at him, then I give his hand a light squeeze. "I want to stay with you, Leon. I really do. There's a lot of good to be done, good that *needs* to be done where the law only holds it back. I want to be a part of that. And I want you."

"I wouldn't have it any other way," he says in a husky tone, bending down and pressing his lips to mine for a long, passionate kiss. "I want you to ride with me, Cherry. Be my girl. My 'old lady'. Official."

"When the law won't do what it takes," I answer, holding his face lovingly, "we will, Leon. Together."

EPILOGUE - CHERRY

"I remember when this place was just an empty lot filled with broken-down car parts and stuff," comments one of Eva's many cousins, whose name I can't place.

"Me, too!" I exclaim. "I used to ride my bike here with my friends and play with the metal scraps. I suppose a park is probably a little safer for the kids, though."

We all laugh, gathered together on checkered blankets and handmade quilts offered earnestly by Wanda Lawrence. The Lawrences are perched at a wooden picnic table nearby, the sweet elderly couple beaming at each other over a basket of cheese and fruit. I smile, leaning into Leon's shoulder. He kisses the side of my head and tugs me closer.

"I'm just glad we were able to make something good come out of this whole ugly mess," Anya says, holding hands with her new boyfriend, none other than the *former* Officer Samuels. After everything that went down, he quit the force and started hanging around the Glass, earning his stripes until he was finally, officially initiated. Ever since the day he threw down his badge and gun, he's been latched to Anya's side. The two of them are an unlikely couple — but he's such a lovable goof that he helps her lighten up and laugh a little. I've never seen her smile as much as she has in the past few months that they've been together. And the Lawrences are over the moon that their former daughter-in-law has found someone who makes her happy. Wanda tells me it's what Henry would've wanted.

"This park is beautiful," Genn comments, leaning back in the grass. "I'm so glad the kids have somewhere cool to hang out now."

"Yeah, and it's nice to see some of the local resources finally taking care of this part of town. God, it used to be such a sad place. Now it hardly looks like the same neighborhood,"

Vasily says. He's standing proudly a few feet away, surveying the park with a grin.

We've all spent the past six months finagling with city planners and gathering the funds to get this park up and running. Hard to believe eight months ago this field was the horrific site of so many shallow, unmarked graves. Such a sad place filled with dark memories — but we refused to let it stay that way. With the assistance of the feds, we've managed to track down the family members of those who were buried here, allowing the families to give their loved ones a proper burial. And now, across the field, there is a beautiful black marble memorial plaque with all their names etched into it with golden lettering. We want to be respectful of those whose lives were carelessly, cruelly squandered away. On the bottom of the list is my dad's name, immortalized.

But that doesn't mean we're going to let this field rot and fester in sadness.

Now, it's home to lovely green grass, an impressive playground, an outdoor barbeque area, several picnic tables, and even a bike trail cut through the surrounding wooded area. The field, first a desolate scrap metal yard, then a heartbreaking crime scene, is now bustling with activity and filled with laughter and love.

I am proud of what we've all accomplished, and I am bursting with joy to think that one day, my own child will play here, too. I wonder if he will be just as daring and determined as his father, or if he will be impossibly curious and loyal as me. I plan to name him John, after my dad. I think I'm finally living up to my potential, carrying out all the dreams my father had for me. Ellen Hardy was impressed with the article I produced about Doyle and Chandler's big scandal, and she has agreed to keep me on staff as a writer and editor — while allowing me to work remotely. I have my big-city dream job, but I still get to live in my beloved hometown!

We've moved back into my dad's old house, and with the help of the Club, Leon and I have given the place a massive makeover — restoring the house to its former glory without losing any of its distinctive, vintage charm. It's just enough to suit the three of us, with room to grow.

Rubbing my swollen belly, I turn to look up into my husband's handsome face. His vivid green eyes meet mine and that same exhilarating thrill passes down my body. I don't think I'll ever stop being amazed by him. I've never known love like this, and I've never been so happy in my entire life. I can't help thinking that all my aimless wandering, my inability to really find my happy place in New York, was all just a series of road signs pointing me back home. I have become a firm believer in fate. Leon and I are a testament to the existence of destiny. After all, he's the one who saved me from drowning so many years ago — but I'd like to think that, in the end, we really saved each other.

GLOSSARY

Kotika - Kitty cat

Nichego - Nothing

Klyanus - I swear

Zasranec - Asshole

Da, da, moy drug - Yes yes, my friend

Podruga - Girlfriend

Politsiya - Police

Khorosho - Alright

Devushka - Girl

Sotrudnik - Officer

Mudak - Asshole/dickhead

Chert voz'mi - Damn it

Byet ostorozhen - Carefully

Zatk'nis, mu'dak - Dumb asshole

Pidarasy - vacation

Vy prekrasny - Beautiful

Obeshchayu - I promise

Ne volnuytes, kroshka - It's okay, baby

Ochyen priyatno, sestra - Nice to meet you, sister

Moy brat - My brother

Bratishka - Little brother

Pozhaluysta - Please

Smelaya devushka - Daring girl

Sestra - Sister

Spasibo - Thank you

Da svidaniya - Goodbye

Fsyevo harosheva - Safe travels

Pizdoon - Fucking liar

ALSO BY ALEXIS ABBOTT

Redeeming Viktor
Most Wanted: Lilly (Novella)
Taken by the Hitman
Hostage of the Hitman
Stolen from the Hitman
Captive of the Hitman
Saved by the Hitman
Sold to the Hitman
Owned by the Hitman
Ruthless
Criminal
Falling for her Boss (Novella)
The Narrow Path
Strayed from the Path
Path to Ruin

ABOUT THE AUTHOR

Alexis Abbott writes about bad boys protecting their girls! With super steamy sex, gritty suspense, and lots of romance, she's a fixture on Amazon's best-seller and all-star lists.

She also writes as Alex Abbott for her erotic thrillers and contemporary romance.

She lives in beautiful St. John's, NL, Canada with her amazing husband.

Join her newsletter for new release information.

http://alexabbottauthor.com/newsletter/

CPSIA information can be obtained
at www.ICGtesting.com
Printed in the USA
LVOW08s2122070917
547939LV00001B/58/P

9 781545 531341